"Mere Friendship Between Us Just Won't Work."

"You don't think so?"

"No." Ian's voice was clipped and confident. "And since things can never be like they were, we need closure to the relationship, a permanent end."

Brooke knew that what he was saying was true, but hearing him say it hurt her deeply.

"So, how do you suggest we go about finding this closure?" she asked. "Do you want me to leave?"

He stared at her for a long moment before answering. "No. I don't want you to leave. What I want, what I need, is to have you out of my system once and for all. I know of only one way to make that happen...."

Dear Reader,

It is with great pleasure that I bring you another Westmoreland's love story. After officially introducing Ian to you in *Riding the Storm*—Storm Westmoreland's story—Ian has constantly been on my mind. I think that it is time for him to turn in his player's card.

I love writing stories of former lovers reuniting, and for Ian I thought this would be the perfect way to mend his wounded heart. He thinks he broke off his affair with Brooke Chamberlain for all the right reasons. But when their paths cross again four years later, he is forced to deal with sexually charged memories and the lingering emotions that he can't put to rest. The question of the hour is, does he really want to? Ian is left wondering if he acted too hastily in ending things with Brooke.

And just like the Westmoreland men before him, Ian has to learn a hard lesson about love—some things are just meant to be.

I hope you enjoy Ian and Brooke's journey back to never-ending love.

Enjoy,

Brenda Jackson

BRENDA JACKSON

Ian's Ultimate Gamble

Published by Silhouette Books
America's Publisher of Contemporary Romance

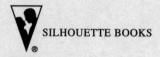 **SILHOUETTE BOOKS**

ISBN-13: 978-0-373-76745-8
ISBN-10:   0-373-76745-5

IAN'S ULTIMATE GAMBLE

Copyright © 2006 by Brenda Streater Jackson

Visit Silhouette Books at www.eHarlequin.com

Printed in U.S.A.

Books by Brenda Jackson

Silhouette Desire

Delaney's Desert Sheikh #1473
A Little Dare #1533
Thorn's Challenge #1552
Scandal between the Sheets #1573
Stone Cold Surrender #1601
Riding the Storm #1625
Jared's Counterfeit Fiancée #1654
Strictly Confidential Attraction #1677
Taking Care of Business #1705
The Chase Is On #1690
The Durango Affair #1727
Ian's Ultimate Gamble #1745

*Westmoreland family titles

Kimani Romance

Solid Soul

BRENDA JACKSON

is a die "heart" romantic who married her childhood sweetheart and still proudly wears the "going steady" ring he gave her when she was fifteen. Because she's always believed in the power of love, Brenda's stories always have happy endings. In her real-life love story, Brenda and her husband live in Jacksonville, Florida, and have two sons.

A *USA TODAY* bestselling author, Brenda divides her time between family, writing and working in management at a major insurance company. You may write Brenda at P.O. Box 28267, Jacksonville, Florida 32226, by e-mail at WriterBJackson@aol.com or visit her Web site at www.brendajackson.net.

To Gerald Jackson, Sr., my husband and hero.

To all my readers who love the Westmorelands.

To my Heavenly Father who gave me
the gift to write.

Happy is the man that findeth wisdom,
and the man that getteth understanding.
—*Proverbs* 3:13

Prologue

"I won't do it, Malcolm!" Brooke Chamberlain said sharply as she absently pushed a dark-brown dread that had fallen in her face back behind her ear. If she'd had any kind of warning of the reason she'd been summoned to her boss's office, she would have found an excuse not to come.

As far as she was concerned what he was asking her to do was totally unacceptable. First, she had just come off one assignment, where a successful vineyard had been caught producing more than vintage wine, and second, he wanted her to go back out west and literally spy on the one man who hated her guts—Ian Westmoreland.

Malcolm Price rubbed a frustrated hand down his face before saying, "Sit down, Brooke, and let me explain why I decided to give the assignment to you."

Brooke gave an unladylike snort. As far as she was concerned there was nothing he could explain. Malcolm was more than just her boss. He was a good friend and had been since their early days with the Bureau when he'd been a fellow agent. Because they had been good friends, he was one of the few people who knew of her past relationship with Ian as well as the reason they had parted ways.

"How can you of all people ask me to do that to Ian, Malcolm?" she said, pacing the room as she spoke, refusing to do as he'd asked and sit down.

"Because if you don't, Walter Thurgood will be assigned to do it."

She stopped moving. "Thurgood?"

"Yes, and once he is, it will be out of my hands."

Brooke sat down in the chair Malcolm had offered her earlier. Walter Thurgood, a hotshot upstart, had been with the Bureau for a couple of years. The man had big goals, and one was to be the top man at the FBI. After several assignments he'd earned the reputation of being one of those agents who got the job done, although there were times when how he'd gone about it had been questionable.

"And even if Ian Westmoreland is clean, by the time Thurgood finishes with him, he'll make him seem like the dirtiest man on this planet if it makes Thurgood look good," Malcolm said with disgust in his voice.

Brooke knew Malcolm was right. And she also knew what Malcolm wasn't saying—that when you were the son of someone already at the top, the people around you were less likely to spank your hand when you behaved improperly.

"But if you think Ian is running a clean operation and you don't suspect him of anything, why the investigation?" she asked.

"Only because the prior owner of the casino, Bruce Aiken, was found guilty of running an illegal betting operation there, and we don't want any of his old friends to come out from whatever rock they hid under during Aiken's trial and start things up again without Westmorland's knowledge. So in a way you'll be doing him a big favor."

Brooke's gaze dropped from Malcolm's to study her hands, clenched in her lap. Ian would not see things that way, and both of them knew it. It would only widen the gap of mistrust between them. But still, she knew there was no way she could allow Thurgood to go in and handle things. It would be downright disastrous for Ian.

She lifted her head and met Malcolm's gaze once again. "And this is not an official investigation?"

"No. You'll be there for a much-needed vacation, while keeping your eyes and ears open."

She leaned forward as anger flared in her eyes. "Ian is one of the most honest men I know."

"In that case you don't have anything to worry about."

She stared at Malcolm thoughtfully for a moment and then said. "Okay."

Malcolm lifted a dark brow. "That means you're going to do it?"

She narrowed her eyes. She was caught between a rock and a hard place and they both knew it. "You knew I would."

He nodded and she saw another certainty in the depths of his dark blue eyes. The knowledge that four years after their breakup she was still in love with Ian Westmoreland.

One

Ian Westmoreland sat at his desk, knee-deep in paperwork, when for no apparent reason he felt a quick tightening in his gut. He was a man who by thirty-three had learned to trust his intuition as well as his deductive reasoning. He lifted his head to glance at the wood-paneled wall in front of him.

He reached out, pressed a button and watched as the paneling slid back to reveal a huge glass wall. The people on the other side who were busy wandering through the casino, taking their chances at the slot machines, gambling tables and arcades, had no idea they were being watched. In certain areas of the casino they were being listened to, as well. More than once the security monitors had picked up conversations best left unheard. But when you operated a casino as large as the Rolling Cascade, the monitors and one-sided mirror were in place for security reasons. Not everyone who came to a casino was there to play. There were those who came to prey on the weaknesses of others, and those were the ones his casino could do without. His huge surveillance room on the third floor, manned by top-notch security experts viewing over a hundred monitors twenty-four hours a day, made sure of it.

Since the grand opening, a lot of people had made reservations merely to check out the newly remodeled casino and resort and to verify the rumors that what had once been a dying casino had been brought back to life in unprecedented style. People Magazine had announced in a special edition that the Rolling Cascade had brought an ambience of Las Vegas to Lake Tahoe and had done it with class, integrity and decorum.

Ian stood and moved around to sit on the corner of his desk, his eyes sharp and assessing as he scanned the crowd. There had to have been a reason he was feeling uptight. The grand opening had been a success and he was glad he'd made the move from riverboat captain to casino owner with ease.

A few minutes later he was about to give up, consider his intuition as having an off day and get back to work, when he saw her.

Brooke Chamberlain.

He stood as his entire body got tense. What the hell was she doing here? Deciding he wasn't going to waste time trying to figure that out, he reached back to the phone on his desk. His call was quickly answered by the casino's security manager.

"Yes, Ian?"

"There's a woman standing at the east-west blackjack table wearing a powder-blue pantsuit. Please escort her to my office immediately."

There was a pause when his security manager asked a question. And in a tight voice Ian responded, "Yes, I know her name. It's Brooke Chamberlain."

After hanging up the phone, his full attention went back to the woman he'd once come pretty damn close to asking to be his wife…before her betrayal. The last time he'd seen her had been three years ago in Atlanta at his cousin Dare's wedding. Since she'd once worked for Sheriff Dare Westmoreland as one of his deputies, she'd been invited, and Ian had deliberately ignored her.

But not this time. She was on his turf and he intended to let her know it.

Ian was watching her.

Brooke wasn't sure from where but the federal agent in her knew how. Video monitors. The place was full of them, positioned so discreetly she doubted the crowd of people who were eager to play the odds knew they were on camera.

"Excuse me, Ms. Chamberlain?"

Brooke turned to stare into the face of a tall, husky-looking man in his late forties with blond hair and dark blue eyes. "Yes?"

"I'm Vance Parker, head of security for the casino. The owner of this establishment, Ian Westmoreland, would like a few words with you in his office."

Brooke's lips curved into a smile. She seriously doubted that Ian had just a "few words" to say to her. "All right, Mr. Parker, lead the way."

And as Vance Parker escorted her to the nearest elevator she prayed that she would be able to survive the next two weeks.

With his gaze glued to the glass, Ian had watched the exchange; had known the exact moment Vance had mentioned his name. Upon hearing it, Brooke's reaction hadn't been one of surprise, which shot to hell the possibility that she hadn't known he owned the place. She had knowingly entered the lion's den, and he was determined to find out why.

He stood and moved around his desk, suddenly feeling that knot in his gut tighten even more. And when he heard the ding, a signal that someone was on their way up in his private elevator, the feeling got worse. Although he didn't want to admit it, he was about to come face-to-face with the one woman he'd never been able to get out of his system. Whether deliberately or otherwise, during the two years they were together, Brooke had raised the bar on his expectations about women. Deputy by day and total woman at night, she had made any female that had followed in her wake seem tremendously lacking. He'd had to finally face the fact that whether he liked it or not, Brooke Chamberlain had been the ultimate woman. The one female who had robbed his appetite for other women. The one woman who'd been able to tame his wild heart.

Not only tame it, but capture it.

The memory brought a bitter smile his lips. But today he was older and wiser, and the heart she once controlled had since turned to stone. Still, that didn't stop his breath from catching in his throat when he turned at the sound of the elevator door opening.

Their gazes connected, and he acknowledged that the chemistry they'd always shared was still there. Hot. Intense. Soul stirring. He felt it, clear across the room, and when he felt the floor shake, he placed his hand on his desk to keep his balance.

This was the closest they'd been to each other since that morning when he'd found out the truth and had walked out of her apartment after their heated argument. At Dare and Shelly's wedding, Ian had kept his distance, refusing to come within ten feet of her, but those gut-wrenching vibes had been strong then, nonetheless.

Over the years it had been hard to let go of the memory of the day they'd met in Dare's office, when she'd been twenty-two. Even in her deputy uniform she had taken his breath away, just as she was doing now at twenty-eight.

Despite their separation and the circumstances that had driven him to end what he'd thought was the perfect love affair, he had to admit that in his opinion she was the most beautiful woman he'd ever set eyes on. She had skin the color of sweet almond; expressive eyes that turned various shades of brown depending on her mood; lips that could curve in a way to make every cell in his body vibrate; and the mass of dreds that came to her shoulders, which he loved holding on to each and every time he entered her body.

His hand balled into a fist at his side. The thought that Brooke could make him dredge up unwanted memories spiked his anger, and he forced his gaze away from her to Vance. "Thanks, Mr. Parker. That will be all."

Ian watched his good friend lift a curious brow and shrug big wide shoulders before turning to get back on the elevator. As soon as the elevator door closed, Ian's attention returned to Brooke. She had moved across the room and was standing with her back to him, staring at a framed photo of him and Tiger Woods and another of him and Dennis Rodman.

She surprised him when she broke the silence by saying, "I heard Tiger and Dennis have homes in this area."

Ian arched a brow. So she wanted to make small talk, did she? He shouldn't have been surprised. Brooke had a tendency to start babbling whenever she was placed in what she considered a nervous situation. He'd actually found it endearing the night of their first date. But now it was annoying as hell.

He didn't want her to make small talk. He didn't want her there, period, which brought him back to the reason she was here in his office. He wanted answers and he wanted them now.

"I didn't have Vance bring you up here to discuss the residences of Woods and Rodman. I want to know what the hell you're doing here, Brooke."

The moment of reckoning had finally arrived. Brooke had grabbed the chance to take her eyes off Ian when he'd all but ordered Vance Parker to leave them alone. Although she had prepared for this moment from the day she'd left Malcolm's office, she still wasn't totally ready for the encounter. Yet there was nothing she could do but turn around and hope that one day, if he ever found out the truth, he would forgive the lie she was about to tell.

On a sigh, she slowly turned, and the moment she did so their eyes locked with more intensity than they had earlier when Vance had been present. Her internal temperature suddenly shot sky high, and every cell in her body felt fried from the sweltering heat that suddenly consumed her.

Words momentarily failed her since Ian had literally taken her breath away. He had always been a good-looking man, and today, three years since she'd seen him last, he was doubly so; especially with the neatly trimmed beard he was sporting. He'd always had that drop-dead-gorgeous and let-me-bed-you-before-I-die look. He'd been a man who'd always been able to grab the attention of women. And now this older Ian was a man who exuded raw, masculine sexuality.

When she had returned to Atlanta to take the job as one of Dare Westmoreland's deputies, she had heard about the two Westmoreland cousins who were the same age and ran together in what women had called a wolf pack. Ian and his cousin Storm had reputations around Atlanta of being ultimate players, the epitome of legendary lovers. Storm had been dubbed the Perfect Storm and Ian, the Perfect End.

It was rumored that any woman who went out with Ian got the perfect ending to their evening, after sharing a bed with him. But all that had changed when he'd begun showing interest in her. He'd called her a hard nut to crack; she'd been one of the few women to rebuff his charm.

Instead of willingly falling under his spell like other women, she'd placed it on him to earn his way into her bed. The result had been two years of being the exclusive recipient of his special brand of sexual expertise.

The rumors hadn't been wrong, but neither had they been completely right. She had discovered that not only was Ian the Perfect End but he was the Perfect Beginning as well. No one could wake a woman up each morning the way he could. The memories of their lovemaking sessions could still curl her toes and wet her panties. He had been her first lover and, she thought further, her only lover.

"Are you going to stand there and say nothing or are you going to answer my question, Brooke?"

Ian's question reclaimed Brooke's attention and reminded her why she was there. And with the angry tone of his voice all the memories they'd ever shared were suddenly crushed. Placing her hands on her hips she answered with the same curt tone he'd used on her. "I'll gladly answer your question, Ian."

Ian folded his arms across his chest. How could he have forgotten how quick fire could leap into her eyes whenever she got angry, or how her full and inviting lips could form one perturbed pout? Over the years he had missed that all-in-your-face, hot-tempered attitude that would flare up whenever she got really mad about something.

The women he'd dated after her had been too meek and mild for his taste. They'd lacked spunk, and if he'd said jump, they would have asked how high. But not the woman standing in front of him. She could dish it out like nobody's business and he had admired her for it. That was probably one of the reasons he had fallen so hard for her.

"The reason I'm here is like everyone else. I needed

time away from my job and decided to check in here for two weeks," she said, intruding into his thoughts.

Ian sighed. As far as he was concerned her reason sounded too pat. "Why here? There are other places you could have gone."

"Yes, and at the time I booked the two weeks I didn't know you were the owner. I thought you were still a riverboat captain."

For a few seconds he said nothing. "Hurricane Katrina brought a temporary end to that. But I'd decided to purchase this place months before then. It was just a matter of time before I came off the river to settle on land."

He studied her for a moment, then asked, "And when did you find out this place was mine?"

Brooke gave a small shrug. "A few days ago, but I figured what the hell, my money spends just as well as anyone else's, and I can't go through life worrying about bumping into you at the next corner."

She released a disgusted sigh and raked her hands through her dreads, making them tumble around her shoulders. "Oh, for heaven's sake, Ian, we have a past, and we should chalk it up as a happy or unhappy time in our lives, depending on how you chose to remember it, and move on. I heard this was a nice place and decided it was just what I needed. And to be quite honest with you I really don't appreciate being summoned up here like I'm some kind of criminal. If you're still stuck on the past and don't think we can share the same air for two weeks let me know and I can take my money elsewhere."

Anger made Ian's jaw twitch. She was right, of course—he should be able to let go and move on;

however, what really griped his insides more than anything was not the fact that they had broken up but why they had. They'd been exclusive lovers. She was the one woman he had considered marrying. But in the end she had been the woman that had broken his heart.

Even when she had moved away to D.C. to take that job with the Bureau, and he had moved to Memphis to operate the *Delta Princess,* they'd been able to maintain a long-distance romance without any problems and had decided within another year to marry.

But the one time she should have trusted him enough to confide in him about something, she hadn't. Instead she had destroyed any trust between them by not letting him know that a case she'd been assigned to investigate had involved one of his business partners. By the time he'd found out the truth, a man had lost his life and a family had been destroyed.

As far as her being here at the Rolling Cascade, he much preferred that she leave. Seeing her again and feeling his reaction to her proved one thing: even after four years she was not quite out of his system and it was time to get her out. Perhaps the first step would be proving they *could* breathe the same air.

"Fine, stay if you want, it's your decision," he finally said.

Brooke lifted her chin. Yes, it would be her decision. There was no doubt in her mind if it was left up to him, he would toss her out on her butt, possibly right smack into Lake Tahoe. "Then I'm staying. Now if you'll excuse me I want to begin enjoying my vacation."

She went to the elevator and without glancing back

at him pushed a button, and when the doors opened she stepped inside. When she turned, their gazes met again, and it was during that brief moment of eye contact before the doors swooshed closed that he thought he saw something flicker in the depths of her dark eyes. Cockiness? Regret? Lust?

Ian drew his brows together sharply. How could he move on and put things behind him when the anger he felt whenever he thought of what she'd done was still as intense as it had always been?

Moving around his desk he pushed a button. Within seconds Vance's deep voice came on the line. "Yes, Ian?"

"Ms. Chamberlain is on her way back down."

"All right. Do you want me to keep an eye on her while she's here?"

"No," Ian said quickly. For some reason the thought of someone else—especially another man—keeping an eye on Brooke didn't sit well with him. Deciding he owed his friend some sort of explanation he said, "Brooke and I have a history we need to bury."

"Figured as much."

"And another thing, Vance. She's a federal agent for the FBI."

Ian heard his friend mutter a curse word under his breath before asking, "She's here for business or pleasure?"

"She claims it's pleasure, but I'm going to keep an eye on her to be sure. For all I know, some case or another might have brought her to these parts, and depending on what, it could mean bad publicity for the Cascade."

"Wouldn't she tell you if she were here on business?"

Ian's chuckle was hard and cold. "No, she wouldn't tell me a damn thing. Loyalty isn't one of Brooke Chamberlain's strong points."

Knowing video monitors were probably watching her every move, Brooke kept her cool as she strolled through the casino to catch the elevator that connected to the suite of villas located in the resort section. All around her crowds were still flowing in, heading toward the bar, the lounge or the area lined with slot machines.

It was only moments later, after opening the door to her villa and going inside, that she gave way to her tears. The look in Ian's dark eyes was quite readable, and knowing he hated her guts was almost too much to bear. If he ever found out the real reason she was there...

She inhaled deeply and wiped her cheeks, knowing she had to check in with Malcolm. Taking the cell phone from her purse, she pressed a couple of buttons. He picked up on the second ring.

"I'm at the Rolling Cascade, Malcolm."

He evidently heard the strain in her voice and said, "I take it that you've seen Ian Westmoreland."

"Yes."

After a brief pause he said, "You know this isn't an official investigation, Brooke. Your job is to enjoy your vacation, but if you happen to see anything of interest to let us know."

"That's still spying."

"Yes, but it's beneficial to Westmoreland. You're there to help him, not hurt him."

"He won't see it that way." Her reply was faint as more

tears filled her eyes. "Look, Malcolm, I'll get back to you if there's anything. Otherwise, I'll see you in two weeks."

"Okay, and take care of yourself."

Brooke clicked off the phone and returned it to her purse. She walked through the living room and glanced around, trying to think about anything other than Ian. The resort was connected to the casino by way of elevators, and the way the villas had been built took advantage of paths for bicyclers and joggers, who thronged the wide wooden boardwalk that ran along the lake's edge. Since this was mid-April and the harsh winter was slowly being left behind, she could imagine many people would be taking advantage of those activities. The view of the mountains was fabulous, and considering all the on-site amenities, this was a very beautiful place.

After taking a tour of her quarters, she felt a combined mixture of pleasure and excitement rush through her veins. Her villa was simply beautiful, and she was certain she had found a small slice of paradise. This was definitely a place to get your groove on.

The view of Lake Tahoe through both her living room and bedroom windows was breathtaking, perfect to capture the striking colors of the sunset. Brooke was convinced the way her villa was situated among several nature trails was the loveliest spot she had ever found. This was a place where someone could come and leave their troubles behind. But for her it was a place that could actually intensify those troubles.

Pushing that thought from her mind, she once again entered her bathroom, still overwhelmed. It was just as large as the living room and resembled a private, tropical spa. This was definitely a romantic retreat, she thought, crossing the room to the Jacuzzi tub, large enough to accommodate four people comfortably. Then there was the trademark that she'd heard was in every bathroom in the villa—a waterfall that cascaded down into a beautiful fountain.

She breathed in deeply, proud of Ian and his accomplishments, and recalled the many nights they would snuggle in bed while he shared his dream of owning such a place with her. When the opportunity came for him to purchase the *Delta Princess,* a riverboat that departed from Memphis on a ten-day excursion along the Mississippi with stops in New Orleans, Baton Rouge, Vicksburg and Natchez, she had been there on his arm at the celebration party his brothers and cousins had thrown. And when his cousin Delaney had married a desert sheikh, she had been the one to attend the weddings with him in both the States and the Middle East.

She sighed, knowing she had to let go of the past the way she'd suggest that he do. But the two years they were together had been good times for her, the best she could have ever shared with anyone, and she had looked forward to the day they would join their lives together as one.

She frowned. Four years ago Ian had refused to hear anything she had to say; had even refused to acknowledge that if the FBI hadn't discovered Boris Knowles's connection to organized crime when they had, all of the man's business dealings would have come under scrutiny, including his partnership with Ian.

Common sense dictated that she tread carefully where Ian was concerned. He was smart and observant.

And he didn't trust her one iota. There was no doubt in her mind that he would be watching her.

Brooke's breathing quickened at the thought of his eyes on her for any amount of time, and moments later a smile curved the corners of her lips. Then she laughed, a low, sultry sound that vibrated through the room. Let him watch her, and while he was doing so maybe it was time to let him know exactly what he'd lost four years ago when he'd walked out of her life.

Ian glanced at the clock on his office wall and decided to give up his pretense of working, since he wasn't concentrating on the reports, anyway. He had too many other things on his mind.

He resisted the urge, as he'd done several times within the past couple of hours, to push the button and see what was going on in the casino, in hopes he would get a glimpse of Brooke. His hand tightened around the paper he held in his hand. He thought he was downright pathetic. And just to think, she was booked for two weeks.

It took him a minute to notice his private line was blinking, and he quickly picked up his phone. "Yes?"

"Ian, how are you?"

He smiled as he recognized Tara's voice. A pediatrician, she was married to his cousin, Thorn, a nationally known motorcycle builder and racer. "Tara, I'm doing fine. And what do I owe the pleasure of this call?"

"Delaney's surprise birthday party. Shelly and I are finalizing the guest list and we wanted to check with you about someone who's on it."

Ian leaned back in his chair. It was hard to believe

that his cousin Delaney would be thirty. Her husband, Prince Jamal Ari Yasir, wanted to give his wife the celebration of a lifetime and he wanted it held at the Rolling Cascade. It seemed only yesterday when he, his brothers and cousins had taken turns keeping an eye on the woman they'd thought at the time was the only female in the Westmoreland family in their generation.

Delaney hadn't made the job easy, and most of the time she'd deliberately been a pain in the ass, but now she was princess of a country called Tahran and mother of the future king. And to top things off, she and Jamal were expecting their second child.

"Who do you want to check with me about?"

"Brooke Chamberlain."

Ian rubbed a hand down his face. Talk about coincidences. Hearing Brooke's name brought a flash of anger. "What about Brooke?"

"I know Delaney would love to see her again, but we thought we'd better check with you. We don't want to make you uncomfortable in any way. I know how things were at Dare and Shelly's wedding."

Ian leaned back in his chair. He doubted anyone knew how difficult things had been for him at that wedding. "Hey, don't worry about it. I can handle it."

There was a slight pause. "You sure?"

"Yes, I'm sure." He decided not to bother mentioning that Brooke was presently in the casino and they were sharing the same air, as she'd put it. "I got over Brooke years ago. She means nothing to me now."

Ian sighed deeply and hoped with all his heart that the words he'd just said were true.

Two

Sitting at a table in the back that afforded him a good view of everything that was going on, Ian saw Brooke the moment she walked into the Blue Lagoon Lounge. Under ordinary circumstances he would have given any other beautiful woman no more than a cursory glance. But unfortunately, not in this case. Brooke was, and always had been, a woman who warranted more than one glance, and her entrance into any room could elicit looks of envy in most women's eyes and a frisson of desire down many men's spines.

Taking a deep breath, he frowned in irritation when he saw the look of heated interest in several masculine gazes as she wove her way through the crowded room with confidence, sophistication and style. And what bothered him more than anything was the fact that the same heated interest in other men's eyes was reflected in his, as well. And her outfit wasn't helping matters. Talk about sexy….

She was wearing her hair up in a knot on her head but had allowed a few strands to fall downward to capitalize on the gracefulness of her neck and the dark lashes that fanned her eyes. And her luscious lips were painted a wicked, flaming-hot red.

But it was that sensuous black number draping her body that had practically every male in the room drooling. Emphasizing every curve as well as those long, beautiful legs, the short dress had splits on both sides, and Ian actually heard the tightening of several male throats when she slid onto a bar stool and exposed a generous amount of thigh. Before she could settle in the seat, he watched as several men stood, eager to hit on her.

Ian took a leisurely sip of his drink. Unless she had changed a lot over the past four years, the poor fools that were all but knocking over chairs to get to her were in for a rude awakening. Although she probably appreciated a hot stare as much as the next female, Brooke was not a woman to fawn over male attention. He had learned that particular lesson the hard way the day they'd met. From that day forward he had never underestimated her as a woman again.

And after being deeply involved with her, he also had a more intimate view of the woman who was the center of every male's attention in the lounge tonight. Without a doubt he was probably the only man in the room who knew about the insecurities that had plagued her through most of her young life. Her father and two older brothers had been known as the Chamberlain Gang, robbing banks as they zigzagged across state lines before the FBI brought an end to their six-month crime spree.

As a teenager, Brooke and her mother had moved to Atlanta to start a new life and find peace from the taunts, ridicule and insensitivity of those less inclined to put the matter to rest. It was then, while in high school, that Brooke decided to bring honor and dignity back to the Chamberlain name by working on the right side of the law.

The activities in the room reclaimed Ian's attention, and he chuckled as one man after another was treated to Brooke's most dazzling smile, followed by her more than courteous refusal. He lifted his drink, and before taking another sip he muttered quietly, "Cheers."

There must be a full moon in the sky, Brooke thought, idly sipping her drink. The wolves were definitely out on the prowl and had erroneously assumed she was an easy prey.

What woman didn't enjoy knowing a man thought she was attractive? But there were some men who thought beauty went hand in hand with stupidity. One man had even offered her the chance to be his second wife, although he claimed he was still happily married to the first.

"I see you haven't lost your touch."

Brooke glanced over at the man who slid into the seat beside her. The smile in his eyes threw her for a second, but that was only after a flutter of awareness inched up her spine. "Thanks. I'll take that as a compliment," she said, sipping her drink when her throat suddenly felt dry.

She fought to keep her body from trembling and, in an attempt at control, studied her reflection in the glass she held instead of placing her full attention on Ian, the way she wanted to do.

"I really thought I wouldn't see you anymore tonight," he said, taking a sip of his own drink.

With that Brooke cocked a brow and turned to him, first taking in how he was dressed. He had changed out of the business suit he was wearing earlier and was wearing another, just as tailormade and just as appealing. And, like the other one, it represented his status as a successful businessman. Whether he wanted to or not, he stood out as the impeccably dressed owner of this casino and was doing so in style.

"Why?" she asked, her concentration moving back to his comment. "Why did you think you wouldn't see me anymore tonight? Did you assume I'd hide out in my villa, Ian, after our meeting earlier? Like I told you, I can't go through life worrying about running into you at every corner like I did something wrong."

Ian's eyes narrowed. "A man's life was lost," he said in a tight voice.

"Yes," she said coolly. "But Boris Knowles should have considered the consequences. He didn't get involved with a group of amateur criminals, Ian. He was involved in organized crime. Don't try and make me feel guilty for the choices he made."

"But had I known, I—"

"Had you known, there wouldn't have been anything you could have done. He was in too deep. Why is it so hard for you to believe that? Telling you would not have changed a thing, other than involve you in a situation you didn't need to be in."

Brooke didn't know what else she could say to get

through that thick skull of his. He refused to believe he wouldn't have made a difference, and that not knowing about Boris had been a blessing.

She heard his muttered curse and knew it was a mistake to have come to the lounge, a place where she figured he would be. "Look, Ian, evidently you and I will always have a difference of opinion about what happened and why I kept things from you. And I'm tired of you thinking I'm the bad guy."

She stood and threw a couple of bills on the counter. "See you around. But then, maybe it would be better if I didn't."

Ian muttered another curse as he watched Brooke disappear through the door, leaving her sensuous scent trailing behind. He felt that familiar stab of pain he encountered whenever he thought of her betrayal. But Brooke's words reminded him of the same thing Dare, a former FBI agent himself, had told him. Organized crime wasn't anything to play with, and regardless of the outcome, Boris had made his choices.

Dare had also tried to make Ian understand that when Brooke had taken the job as a federal agent, she had also made an oath to uphold the law and to maintain a rigid vow of confidentiality. Had she told him about the case, and security had been breached, it would have risked not only Brooke's life but the lives of other federal agents.

Ian had understood all of that, but still, he believed that when two people were committed to each other, there weren't supposed to be any secrets between them. So in his mind she had made a choice between her job and him. That, in a nutshell, was what grated him the most. Yet at some point he had to let go and move on or the bitterness would do him in. He couldn't continue to make her feel like a "bad" guy, especially when he of all people knew how much becoming an agent had meant to her. Twice her application had been turned down when background checks had revealed her family history—namely her father and brothers. It had taken Dare, who'd still maintained close contacts within the Bureau, to write a sterling letter of recommendation to get her in.

Ian pulled in a deep breath. It was time for him and Brooke to finally make peace. He knew that because of all that had happened between them, the love they once shared could never be recovered, but it was time he put his animosity to rest and make an attempt at being friends.

Brooke angrily stripped out of her dress. Ian Westmoreland was as stubborn as any mule could get. He refused to consider that she had been doing her job four years ago and if she had told him anything about the case, her own life could have been in jeopardy. No, all he thought about was what had happened to a man who'd been living a lie to his family, friends and business associates.

Fine, if that was the position Ian wanted to take, even after four years, let him. She refused to allow him to get on her nerves, and somehow and in some way she would wipe away the memories she found almost impossible to part with. More than anything she had to somehow eradicate him from her heart. But in the meantime she planned to enjoy herself for the next two weeks and wouldn't let him stand in the way of her doing just that.

She slipped into the two-piece bathing suit, thinking a late-night swim might make her feel better. Swimming had always relaxed her, and she was seriously considering adding a pool to her home in D.C. The question was whether or not she would have the time to enjoy it. In a few months she would have made her five-year mark with the Bureau and it was time to decide if she wanted to remain out in the field or start performing administrative duties. Her good friend and mentor, Dare Westmoreland, had cautioned her regarding Bureau burnout, which was what had happened to him after seven years as an agent.

Brooke had just grabbed her wrap when she heard the knock at her door. Evidently room service had made a mistake and was at the wrong villa. Making her way across the room, she leaned against the door and glanced through the peephole, and suddenly felt a sensation deep in the pit of her stomach. Her late-night caller was Ian.

She tensed and shook her head. If he thought he would get in the last word he had another thought coming. After removing the security lock she angrily snatched open the door. "Look, Ian, I—"

Before she could finish, he placed a single white rose in her hand. "I come in peace, Brooke. And you're right. It's time to put the past behind us and move on."

Ian's heart slammed against his chest. He had been prepared for a lot of things, but he hadn't been prepared for Brooke to open the door in a two-piece bathing suit with a crocheted shawl wrapped around her waist that didn't hide much of anything.

There were her full, firm breasts that almost poured

out of her bikini top and a tiny waist that flared to shapely hips attached to the most gorgeous pair of legs any woman could possess. And her feet—how could he possibly forget her sexy feet? They were bare, with brightly painted toenails, encased in a pair of cute flat leather sandals.

Her unique scent was feminine and provocative and the same one he had followed out of the lounge. It was the same scent that was filling her doorway, saturating the air surrounding him, getting into his skin. She was and had always been a woman of whom fantasies were made. And seeing her standing there was overwhelming his sense of self-control.

He sighed deeply, inwardly wishing he could focus on something other than her body and her scent. He wanted to concentrate on something like the rose he had given her, but instead his gaze lowered to her navel, which used to be one of his favorite spots on her body. He could recall all the attention he used to give it before moving lower to…

"Ian?"

He snatched his attention back to her face and cleared his throat. Damn, he had come to make peace, not make love. They would never share that type of relationship again. "Yes?"

"Thanks for the rose, and I'm glad we can move forward in our lives, and I hope that one day we can be friends again," she said.

Brooke was watching his eyes, probably noting the caution within their dark depths when he said, "I hope so, too."

She nodded. "Good."

He leaned in the doorway. "You're going out?"

"Yes, I thought I'd go for a swim at one of the pools. The one with the huge waterfall looks inviting."

Ian nodded. It was. He had passed the area on his way here, and another thing he noted was that it was crowded with more men than women. He then remembered that the Rolling Cascade was hosting a convention of the International Association of Electricians. There were over eight hundred attendees, eighty percent of them men who probably thought they were capable of finding a woman's hot spot and wiring her up in a minute flat. He drew his dark brows together sharply. Not with this woman.

"That pool is nice, but I know of one that's a hundred times better," he said, when an idea suddenly popped into his head.

"Really, where?"

"My penthouse."

She met his eyes then, and he could imagine what thoughts were going through her mind. Hell, he was wondering about it himself. He had no right to feel possessive, as if she was still his. But just because she wasn't didn't mean he shouldn't have a protective instinct where she was concerned, did it?

Feeling better about the reason he was inviting her to his suite, he reached out and took her hand in his. "Look, it was just an invitation for you to use my private pool. Besides, I'd like to catch up on how things have been going for you. But if you prefer we don't go any further than the rose, that's fine."

Brooke took a second to absorb Ian's words. He wanted them to become friends again and nothing more. He had given her a peace offering and now he wanted them to catch up on what had been going on in their lives. She doubted that he knew she asked about him often, whenever she and Dare spoke on the phone. She knew Ian was back at the top of his game, had reinstated his role of the Perfect End and now claimed he would never, ever settle down and marry. With his cousin Storm happily married, Ian much preferred being the remaining lone wolf of the Westmoreland clan.

"I'd love to go swimming in your private pool and visit," she said, and hoped and prayed she could get through an evening alone with him in his private quarters.

The smile that touched his lips sent heat spreading through her. "Good. Are you ready to leave now?"

"Yes. I just need to grab a towel."

"Don't bother. I have plenty."

"Okay, let me get my door key."

Moments later she stepped out and closed the door behind her. As they walked together, side by side, toward a bank of elevators, she was fully aware that Ian was looking at her, but she refused to look back. If for one instant she saw heated desire in his eyes, she would probably do something really stupid like give in to the urgency of the sexual chemistry that always surrounded them and ask him to kiss her. But knowing what ironclad control Ian could have, he would probably turn her down.

"Welcome to my lair, Brooke Chamberlain."

Ian stepped aside to let her enter, and Brooke's breath caught the moment she stepped into the room. His personal living quarters was a floor above his office, and both were connected by a private elevator, an arrangement he found convenient.

The moment Brooke crossed over the threshold it was if she had walked into paradise. She had figured that, as the owner of the Rolling Cascade, Ian would have a nice place, but she hadn't counted on anything this magnificent, this breathtaking.

His appreciation of nature was reflected in the numerous plants strategically arranged in the penthouse, which encompassed two floors connected by a spiral staircase.

The first things she noticed were the large windows and high ceilings, as well as the penthouse's eclectic color scheme—a vibrant mix of red, yellow, orange, green and blue. She was surprised at how well the colors worked together. For symmetry, the two fireplaces in the room were painted white, and then topped with drapery of a hand-painted design.

It appeared the furniture had been designed with comfort in mind, and several tropical-looking plants and trees gave sections of the room a garden effect.

"Come on, let me show you around," he said, taking her hand in his.

The warmth of the strong hand encompassing hers sent a sea of sensation rippling through her. She tried not to think about what expert hands they were and how he used to take his thumb and trail it over her flesh, starting at her breasts and working his way downward, sometimes alternating his thumb with his tongue.

His silky touch could make her purr, squirm, and elicited all kind of sounds from her. And when he would work his way to her navel—heaven help her—total awareness for him would consume her entire body, making her breathe out his name in an uncontrolled response to his intimate ministrations.

"You okay?"

His words snatched her back from memory lane, and she glanced up at him. "Yes, why do you ask?"

"No reason," he murmured, and the tone sent a shiver all through her.

Brooke raised a brow. Had she given something away? Had she made a sound? One he recognized? One he remembered?

They walked together while he gave her a tour. French doors provided a gracious entry from room to room, and the kitchen, with its state-of-the-art cabinets and generously sized island, showed a comfortable use of space. The skill of an interior designer touched every inch of Ian's home, and Brooke thought this was definitely the largest penthouse she'd ever seen. It encompassed more square footage than her house back in D.C.

Ian told her that Prince Jamal Ari Yasir was his primary investor and that Ian's brothers, Spencer and Jared, and his cousin Thorn had also invested in the Rolling Cascade. The one thing Brooke had always admired about the Westmoreland family was their closeness and the way they supported each other.

When he showed her his bedroom a spurt of envy ran through Brooke at the thought of the other women who'd shared the king-size bed with him. But then she quickly reminded herself that Ian's love life was no business of hers.

"So, what do you think?" he asked casually.

His question momentarily froze her, and she shifted

her eyes from the bed and met his gaze. "I'm really proud of you, Ian, of all your accomplishments. And you are blessed to belong to a family that fully supports what you do. They are really super."

Ian smiled. "Yes, they are."

"And how are your parents?"

"They're doing fine. You do know that Storm got married?" he asked, leading her out of the bedroom, down the spiral stairs, to an area that led toward an enclosed pool.

She smiled up at him. "Yes. I can't imagine marriage for the Perfect Storm."

The corners of Ian lips curled in a smile. "Now he's the Perfect Dad. His wife Jayla and their twin daughters are the best things that ever happened to him. He loves them very much."

When there was a lull in the conversation, Brooke said, "And I heard about your uncle Corey's triplets."

He chuckled. "Yeah, can you believe it? He found out an old girlfriend had given birth to triplets around the same time he was united with a woman who'd always been his true love. He's married now and is a very happy man on his mountain."

Brooke nodded. She had visited Corey's Mountain in Montana with Ian and knew how beautiful it was. "I also heard that Chase got married and so did Durango."

He nodded, grinning. "Yes, both were shockers. Chase and Durango married two sisters, Jessica and Savannah Claiborne. Durango and Savannah eloped and held their wedding here."

He then looked over at her. "I see Dare's been pretty much keeping you informed."

She shrugged. She detected a smile in his voice, although she didn't see one in his face. "Yes. Do you resent knowing Dare and I keep in touch?"

"No, not at all," he said, his tone making it seem as if such a notion was ridiculous. "Dare knew you for a lot longer than I did. You used to be his deputy and the two of you were close. I didn't expect you to end your relationship with him just because things didn't work out between us, Brooke. The Westmorelands don't operate that way."

Moments later he added, "And I also know that you've kept in touch with other family members." He shook his head, grinning. "Or should I say they kept up with you. Delaney let me know in no uncertain terms that our breakup had no bearing on your friendship."

"Did she?" Brooke asked, attempting to conjure an air of nonchalance she was far from feeling. She and Delaney had remained friends, and a few years ago when Delaney had accompanied her husband to an important international summit in Washington, the two of them had spent the day shopping, going to a movie and sharing dinner.

"Here we are."

They stopped walking, and Brooke's breath caught. Now this was paradise. Ian's enclosed pool was huge, including a cascading waterfall and several tropical plants, and connecting to his own personal fitness center and games room.

"You like it?"

"Oh, Ian, it's wonderful, and you're right—it's better than the one by the villas."

He reached behind her and handed her a couple of towels off a stack. "Here you are, and I meant to ask earlier, how's your mom?"

Brooke smiled. "Mom's doing fine. Marriage agrees with her. While Dad was living—even though he was incarcerated—she refused to get involved with anyone. She was intent on honoring her wedding vows to him although she'd always deserved better. She refused to divorce him."

Ian nodded. "I heard about your father. I'm sorry."

Brooke shrugged. "He was a couple of years from being up for parole and what does he do?" she asked angrily. "He causes a prison riot that not only cost him his own life but the lives of four other inmates, as well."

"And how are your brothers?"

"Bud and Sam are okay. Mom stays in contact with them more than their biological mother," she said of her father's first wife. When her mother had married Nelson Chamberlain, her brothers were already in their teens.

"I write them all the time and have taken Mom to see them on occasion. I think they've finally learned their lessons and will be ready for parole when the time comes," she said.

Brooke appreciated Ian asking about her family. She had loved her dad and her brothers even though they had chosen lives of crime. And she simply adored her mother for having had the strength to leave her husband to provide her daughter with a better environment.

She was about to remove her wrap when she nervously glanced over at Ian. "Will you be taking a swim, too?"

He smiled, shaking his head. "No, not tonight. The pool will be all yours. There are a couple of calls I need to make, so I'm going to leave you alone for a while. Do you mind?"

"No, and I appreciate you letting me use your pool."

"Don't mention it."

"And I enjoyed our chat, Ian."

"So did I." He glanced at his watch. "I'll be back in around an hour to walk you to your villa."

"All right."

After Ian left, Brooke licked her suddenly dry lips, remembering how quickly he had exited the room. Was she imagining things? Had the thought of her undressing in front of him—doing something of as little significance as removing the wrap of her bathing suit—sent Ian running? Um. Maybe that ironclad control he used to have wasn't as strong as she'd thought.

The possibility that the attraction they'd once shared was just as deep as before sent a warm feeling flowing through her. And suddenly feeling giddy, she removed her wrap, walked over to the deep end of the pool and dived in.

Ian's hand trembled as he poured wine into his glass. Talk about needing a drink. It had taken everything within him not to pull Brooke into his arms at several points during their conversation. And even worse, he had picked up on that vibe, the same one she always emitted whenever she wanted him to make love to her.

It had been awkward to stand beside her and know what her body wanted and not oblige her the way he would have done in the past. Angrily he slammed down the glass on his coffee table. *This is not the past, this is the present and don't even think about going back there, Westmoreland. The only thing you and Brooke can ever be is friends, and even that is really pushing it.*

He muttered a curse, and at the same time the phone rang. It was his private line. "Yes?"

"Hey, you're okay?"

Hearing his cousin Storm's voice, Ian shook his head and smiled. It had always been the weirdest thing. His brother Quade was his fraternal twin like Chase was Storm's. But when it came to that special bond he'd heard that twins shared, it had always been he and Storm and Quade and Chase.

Quade worked for the Secret Service, and half the time none of the family knew what he doing or where he was. But they could depend on Chase to know if Quade was ever in trouble with that special link they shared. Likewise, Ian knew that only Storm could detect when something was bothering him, even thousands of miles away.

"And what makes you think something is wrong?" Ian asked, sitting down on a leather sofa. This spot gave him a view of Brooke whenever she swam in the shallow end of his pool.

Storm chuckled. "Hey, I feel you, man. The one night I should be getting a good night's sleep, now that the girls are sleeping through the night, I'm worried about you."

Ian lifted a brow. "Worried about me?"

"Yes. What's going on, Ian? What has you so uptight that I can sense it?"

Ian's attention was momentarily pulled away from his phone conversation when Brooke swam to the shallow end of the pool. He shifted slightly on the sofa to get a better view and knew from where he sat that he could see her but she couldn't see him.

He watched as she stood up, emerging from the water like a sex goddess as she tossed her wet hair back from her face. But it wasn't her hair that was holding his attention. *Have mercy!* She had a body that made men drool, curves in all the right places—and he was familiar with those curves, every delectable inch. And that bikini, wet and clinging to her, looked good on her. Too good. He could only imagine the reaction she would have gotten from other men. But just the thought that he had once touched her all over, licked her all over, made love to that body in more ways than he could count, sent blood surging through his veins. "Damn."

"Hey, man. Talk to me. What's going on?"

Storm's words reminded Ian he was still holding the phone in his hand, and it was taking every ounce of strength he had to continue to do so. He suddenly felt weak, physically drained.

"Brooke," he finally said, whispering her name softly, drawing out the sound deep from within his throat on a husky sigh. "She's here."

"What do you mean she's there?"

Ian rolled his eyes upward. "Just what I said, Storm. She checked into the Rolling Cascade for two weeks for some R and R. But at this moment she happens to be in my penthouse, using my pool. We're trying to put the past behind us."

"Brilliant. That's just brilliant, Ian," Storm chuckled. "Don't tell me, let me guess. You and Brooke are trying to put the past behind you and become friends. Come on, Ian. Think about it. Do you actually believe you can be just friends with the only woman who's ever had your heart?"

Ian frowned. "Yes, since the key word here is *had*. I stopped loving Brooke years ago."

"So you say."

"So I mean. Good night, Storm."

Three

Ian stood and walked across the room to the wall-to-wall, floor-to-ceiling window that gave a breathtaking view of Lake Tahoe.

When he had reopened the casino after extensive remodeling, he'd given it more than just a new name and a new face. He had given the place a new attitude. He had painstakingly combined the charm of the Nevada landscape with the grandeur of a world-class casino, then added an upscale nightlife whose unique ambiance appealed to a sophisticated clientele.

His penthouse had the best view of the lake. Strategically set on the west side of the casino and covering portions of both the eighth and ninth floors, his domain was away from the villas, the various shops and restaurants, the golf courses with cascading waterfalls and the tennis courts. He considered his personal quarters as his very own private hot spot, although between the hours he'd spent making sure things were perfect for the grand opening nine months ago, his time had been too consumed in business matters to pursue any intimate pleasures, and he had not yet invited a woman up to his lair, other than members of his family and now Brooke.

Brooke.

He cocked his head, and a smile touched his lips when he heard the sound of her splashing around in the pool. For some reason, he liked knowing she was there, and regardless of what Storm thought, he and Brooke held no emotional ties. The most they could ever be again was friends.

Brooke swam back and forth through the calming water as she did another lap around Ian's pool. After several more laps she pulled herself up on the ledge thinking that she'd had a wonderful workout. She felt rejuvenated in one sense and exhausted in another. Beside the pool was a long padded bench that looked absolutely inviting, and she decided to rest a while.

She lay flat on her back and stared up at the ceiling. All she could think about was Ian's dark eyes and the way they had looked at her moments before he'd left her alone. Swim or no swim, she'd been fantasizing about him ever since. She was trying to keep a part of herself distanced; especially knowing how quickly she could be consumed by desire for him. Though she hadn't been completely honest with him about the real reason she was there, she couldn't control her attraction to him. Basic urges were exactly what they were. Basic. And she knew firsthand how skilled Ian was in taking care of anything that ailed her.

She flipped onto her stomach and studied a nearby plant. Anything to get Ian off her mind. But it wasn't working. As her eyes closed, her mind shifted back to a time when he had moved his mouth all over her breasts, sucking and lapping at her nipples while his fingers skimmed just beneath her panties....

Ian wasn't sure how long he stood at the window looking out, idly sipping his wine while seeing various yachts, sailboats and schooners cruising the lake, resembling fireflies below as they went by. Tomorrow was another busy day. He had meetings with Nolen McIntosh, his casino manager, Vance on security matters and Danielle on PR. Then of course there was that discussion with his event planner regarding the final details for Delaney's surprise birthday party.

It took Ian only a minute to notice something was different. There was no sound coming from the pool. He set his wineglass on a nearby table, moved away from the window and headed toward the room where he'd left Brooke almost an hour earlier.

The pool was empty, so he glanced around the room and then saw her. She lay flat on her stomach on the padded leather bench, asleep. The intensity of the emotions he felt at that moment hit him from every angle. When was the last time Brooke had slept at his place? It had been years. Their angry parting words—mostly from him—still burned fervently in his veins. She had tried to explain; tried presenting her side of things. But he hadn't wanted to listen. He hadn't wanted to ever see or talk to her again.

So what was happening here? Why was he talking to

her, seeing her again? Why had he allowed her to invade his space, the only place free of his memories of her?

She moaned in her sleep, and hearing the sound he stepped closer, allowing his gaze to rake over her shapely body, feeling a rush of adrenaline. A deep swallow made its way down his throat as his gaze moved to the tie that held the top part of her bikini in place, the smooth curve of her back, the flare of her hips beneath the thin scrap of material that was supposed to be a bikini bottom. Her skin looked soft, inviting and warm to the touch. He wanted his hands all over her thighs, and he would do anything to cup her delicious bottom. And he didn't want to think about how he wanted to use his mouth on her breasts.

He sighed deeply. Considering their history, it was only natural that he would feel this heated lust, this mind-searing desire. There was a time when, if he'd found her like this, he could have awakened her by making love to her, gently flipping her on her back and using his hands and his mouth to show her what real moans were all about. His stomach begin trembling at the memories, and hot liquid fire filled his body at the very thought. But he knew things were different. They no longer had that kind of relationship, and he doubted they ever would again. She was no longer his to touch at will.

That realization dictated his next move. Reaching to a table behind him he grabbed a huge towel and gently covered her. He would not wake her. He would let her rest. But neither would he leave her. He wanted to be there when she awoke. Call it pure torture, but he wanted to look into the depth of those eyes, catch her drowsy, sleepy, tousled look, the sexy one she got whenever she was rousing from sleep. That look used to stir up every-thing male within him and arouse him to no end. And that look would drive him to take her with a passion that could never be duplicated with any other woman.

Removing his jacket, he folded it neatly and placed it across the back of a wicker sofa before settling down in a wicker chair and stretching his legs out in front of him. From this position he could to watch her while she slept and see her when she woke up.

And as he sat there, his mind went back to that day six years ago when they had met. He had walked into Dare's office, and from that day on his life had never been the same.

Slowly released from the throes of a deep sleep, Brooke kept her eyes closed as she drowsily inhaled gently and then yawned. There was nothing like a swim to work the aches and pains out of her muscles, and that thought made her recall where she was and why the familiar scent of one particular man was surrounding her.

She slowly opened her eyes and they immediately connected to the dark penetrating ones of Ian West-moreland. Sitting in a chair across the room, he looked slightly disheveled, as if he'd been sitting there for a while, but nothing could erase that sexy look he wore so well. What had been a crisp white shirt now had a few buttons undone, and the sleeves were rolled up. With his legs stretched out in front of him, his trousers were pulled tight against muscular, well-defined thighs.

A sensual shiver ran down her body and she felt the huge towel covering her and knew he had placed it there. The thought of him being that close to her, placing a covering over her body, stoked her insides, creating a heavy warmth.

A part of her wanted to sit up, stretch her legs, apologize for falling asleep, but she couldn't do any of those things. She couldn't move; could barely breathe. His gaze was holding her in place and making her remember happier times, passionate times, and she wondered if he was doing the same.

She watched his eyes darken even more, and in response a rush of hormones that had lain dormant for four years rushed through her system. Liquid awareness churned in her stomach, and her entire body suddenly felt sensitive, acutely aware of him as a man. However, not just as any man.

He was the man who had first introduced her to the pleasures that a couple could share; the man who used to wake her up each morning by using his hands and lips on every part of her body; a man who, besides being the best lover any woman could possibly have, had become her confidant and her best friend.

Brooke blinked, was caught momentarily off guard when he stood and began walking toward her, showing telltale proof of how much he wanted her. The bulge in his pants couldn't lie. Her body instantly responded, recognizing the sexual chemistry that emanated from him and quickly overpowered her.

She raised her body to a sitting position, stretched out her legs and braced her hands on both sides of her. She couldn't help wondering what he was thinking. She definitely knew her thoughts. The heated look in his eyes, the hot familiarity, gave her an idea. There was still a lot unsettled between them. There were some things that could never be as they used to be. But there would always be a level where they would be in accord. And this was it.

Deep down a part of her wished otherwise; wished she could expunge him from her heart as she knew he had done her. He might still want her, desire her, but he no longer loved her. But right now, at this moment, heaven help her, it didn't matter. She needed to feel his body pressed close to hers, she needed to once again feel his arms holding her, his mouth tasting hers.

He came to a stop in front of her and the light that poured down from overhead highlighted the darkness of his skin in contrast to his white shirt. She stared up at him, as blood throbbed through her veins, and she took in his broad chest and strong lean body.

She slowly stood, wondering if her legs could hold her weight, but that concern quickly vanished from her mind when she heard a sensual moan escape through his clenched teeth, and she knew he was trying to resist her, fight what they were both feeling.

But when he began to lean closer, she knew he had given up the battle and was giving in to temptation. Common sense was being overwhelmed by lust. And when their mouths connected and their tongues mingled, flames sparked inside of her and she completely lost whatever control she'd had. This is Ian, her mind and body taunted. And she did what seemed so natural, which was to kiss him back in all the ways he had taught her to.

Ian made love to Brooke's mouth with as much skill as he possessed. *Mercy.* He wanted this. He needed this.

Four years hadn't eliminated the yearning, the urgency or the hunger. She wasn't out of his system, and maybe this would be the first step in ridding her from it. But the more their tongues consorted, fused and intertwined, the harder it was to regain control. And when he brought her body closer to his, let his hands slide over her backside with a possessiveness he had no right to feel, he wanted to do more than taste her. He wanted to place her back on the bench, further stroke the heat between them, remove his clothes, straddle her body, remove her bikini bottom and make her his again.

His again.

That thought made him lift his head sharply, knowing that was the last thing he wanted. Things could never go back to being the way they were. He refused to let them. There were some things you could never recover from, and one was a broken heart. He'd loved and he'd loved hard. And whether she had intended to or not, she had destroyed that love.

He looked down and his gaze swept over her features. His eyes touched each and every part of the face he would always cherish. But that was as far as things would ever go. He would want her, lust after her, but he would never love her again.

"Come on and let me walk you back to your villa," he said in a husky voice tinged with regret.

As if he had kissed any and every word from her mouth, Brooke merely nodded, gathered the towel around her and followed him as he led her to his private elevator.

"I didn't mean to overstay my welcome," she finally was able to say when the elevator doors opened.

He looked down at her, his features tight. "You didn't."

For some reason she didn't believe him. One thing she knew about Ian was that he was a man who didn't forgive easily, nor was he quick to forget. He claimed he wanted them to move on and be friends, but she wondered if that's what he really wanted, or if that was something he would ever be willing to tolerate. Brooke opened her mouth to say something and then closed it. Chances were he would be keeping his distance for the remainder of her stay.

When they reached her door he stepped aside to let her unlock it. She thought this was where he would tell her good-night, and he surprised her when he took her hand and followed her inside, closing the door behind him.

"Hidden video cameras in the halls," he whispered in a throaty voice before gently pulling her into his arms. He then leaned down and kissed her again, the connection slow and lingering, but just as thorough as before. The kiss sent shudders all through her.

Moments later his mouth left hers to trail heated kisses along her neck and jaw. The feel of his beard rubbing against her skin was eliciting sensations deep in the pit of her stomach. A man like Ian was deadly in more ways than one.

"Will you go sailing with me tomorrow, Brooke?"

She raised her chin, still shuddering, surprised at his request. "Are you sure that's what you want?" she asked.

He was silent for a moment and stared deep into her eyes. It was all Brooke could do not to melt right there on the spot from the heat generating in his gaze. "Yes, I'm sure." He stepped back. "I'm beginning to realize something, Brooke."

"What?" she asked, having a difficult time swallowing.

"Moving beyond what we once shared isn't going to be as easy as I thought."

She lifted her brow and fought back the thick lump of emotion that clogged her throat, almost kept her from breathing. "What do you mean?"

"Mere friendship between us won't ever work."

"You don't think so?"

"No." His voice was clipped, cool and confident. "And since things can never be like they were, we need finality. Closure. A permanent end."

She knew that what he was saying was true, considering the kisses they had shared, but still, hearing him say it hurt deeply. "So, how do you suggest we go about it? Do you want me to leave?" she asked, knowing that wasn't an option even if he wanted her to.

He stared at her for a long moment, then answered by saying, "No. I don't want you to leave. What I want, what I need, is to have you out of my system, and I know of only one way that can be accomplished."

Brooke sighed deeply. She knew of only one way that could be accomplished, as well, and she wasn't going for it. It might get her out of his system, but it would only embed him deeper into hers.

She shook her head vehemently. "It won't work."

"Trust me, it will."

She lifted her chin and glared at him, trying to ignore the way her inner muscles clenched in response to the huskiness of his voice. "It might work for you, but not for me."

Ian leaned in closer to her, his voice low and deep, his lips just a hair away from touching hers. "I'd love to prove you wrong, Brooke. Even now you feel it, the heat, the urge, the cravings. You remember how things used to be between us as much as I do. You remember our out-of-control hormones, wild nights when we couldn't wait to make love, going so far as to start stripping naked as soon as the door closed behind us."

"Ian."

"And how I would take you right then and there, wherever—on the wall, the floor, the sofa, giving you everything you wanted, whatever you needed. And how you would practically—"

"Stop it, Ian," she said sharply, stepping back away from him to halt the trembling that had begun in her stomach. "I won't let what you're suggesting happen."

She read his expression, saw the challenge in his eyes, the deep-rooted stubbornness. "Okay," he said with a smile that said he didn't believe her any more than she believed herself. "I'll be by to pick you up to go sailing at noon. See you later, Brooke."

Brooke tilted her head, watched him cross the room, open the door and walk out without looking back. She pulled the towel tighter around her body when a chill touched it. After spending so much time in the pool tonight she should be smelling of chlorine. But she smelled of Ian. His manly scent seemed to be all over her.

She dropped the towel and quickly moved toward her bathroom, needing a shower. She would send him a message, letting him know she had changed her mind about going sailing with him.

He might like the idea of playing with fire, but she did not.

Four

"We have reason to believe one of our guests is smoking in his room," Joanne Sutherlin, resort manager, said to the employees around the conference table during the resort's regular status meeting.

"We haven't been able to find any proof, but a housekeeper reports she's smelled smoke. It seems the guest has been trying to disguise his smoking by spraying heavy cologne in the air," she said.

"If we can prove he's breaking a hotel policy, then we can end his stay with us."

Everyone at the table nodded. They knew Ian had very low tolerance when it came to anyone not abiding by the Rolling Cascade's smoke-free policy.

The next item up for discussion by the management team was entertainment. The activities director confirmed that he had booked deals with top performers for the next eighteen months. Highlights of the upcoming schedule included a two-week billing for Mariah Carey in June, Michael MacDonald in September and Phil Collins in December. Smokey Robinson opened tonight in a two-week engagement that was already sold out for every night of the event.

Nolen, the casino manager, indicated security had alerted him that a couple of prostitutes had tried peddling their wares in the casino. Although Nevada had legalized prostitution, it was only allowable within a licensed brothel. Unfortunately, casinos were a prime target for call girls looking for potential "dates." Ian was committed to keeping the Rolling Cascade prostitute free.

"We have the matter taken care of," Nolan assured him.

Ian nodded. That's what he wanted to hear. He glanced at his watch. He had ordered a picnic basket from one of the restaurants for his lunch date with Brooke. He had left a message for her that he would be picking her up at noon and couldn't wait to get her on his boat.

He remembered their conversation last night. He had deliberately walked out the door without looking back. To say he had ruffled a few of her feathers would be an understatement. But then, he had merely been up-front with her. It was too late to start playing games. He knew what they needed and she did as well. In order to bring closure, they needed to expunge each other from their systems, and until that was done there would always be this emotional tug-of-war between them.

He suddenly felt goose bumps cover his body at the thought of seeing her again and of the afternoon he had planned. A hint of a smile tugged at his lips. She might be one resistant female now, but once he got her on his sailboat and made her remember all the stimulating things she was trying to forget, their day would end the way they both wanted it to.

His pulse began beating wildly an hour later as the status meeting ended. He quickly headed toward his penthouse to change into more comfortable clothes.

"Mr. Westmoreland?"

He turned before stepping into his private elevator. "Yes?" he asked Cassie, a young woman who worked in the resort's business center.

"This message was left for you this morning."

He took the sealed envelope she handed him. "Thank you." He tore it open and read the note.

I've changed my mind about going sailing with you, Brooke.

Ian frowned. If Brooke thought she could dismiss him just like that, she had another thought coming.

"Is there anything you need me to do, sir?"

It was then that Ian realized Cassie was still standing there. He lifted his head and met her gaze. This wasn't the first time he'd seen the heated look of lust in the depths of her dark eyes, and he could recognize a flirtatious comment when he heard one. He recalled what he knew about her. She was a recent college graduate with a degree in hotel management. He had decided long ago, after operating his riverboat, that he would never become sexually involved with his employees. And even though, due to his busy schedule, it had been almost a year since he'd slept with anyone, the only woman his body craved had just canceled their lunch date.

* * *

Brooke propped a hand on her hip and stared at the outfits she had placed on the bed. Both were suitable for an afternoon of shopping, but which one should she wear?

The capri pant set was what she would have worn had she gone sailing with Ian. It had a bit more style than the cotton shorts set, and was a designer outfit she'd purchased while in San Francisco last month. The shorts set would provide better comfort of movement as she walked from store to store making purchases. She was about to hang the capri set back in her closet when she heard a knock on her door.

Leaving her bedroom, she wondered if it was housekeeping. The lady had come earlier, but since Brooke had ordered room service for breakfast she had asked the woman to come back later.

Brooke didn't want to think of herself as a coward, but she had dined in her room this morning because she hadn't wanted to run into Ian. They needed at least a couple of days of distance for him to rethink that preposterous suggestion he'd made. In the meantime she would avoid him by taking advantage of all the amenities the resort had to offer. He needed time to cool off, and the interlude would give her the opportunity to asses his operation.

She glanced out the peephole and her heart slammed against her ribs the moment she did so. It was Ian. Did he not get her message canceling their date to go sailing?

When she opened the door, she wasn't quite ready for the fluttering sensation she felt in her chest. He stood in the doorway casually dressed in a pair of khakis and a blue polo shirt and holding a picnic basket. She'd forgotten how good he looked in everyday clothes. He looked sexy in a suit, but in casual wear he was drop-dead gorgeous.

"You ready?" he asked, cutting into her thoughts.

She raised a brow and pulled her robe tighter around her. "Didn't you get my message?"

He smiled as he walked around her, entering the room without an invitation. "Yes, I got it, but I assumed there must have been a mistake."

She glared at him, wondering why he would think that. "Well, you assumed wrong. There is no mistake. I'm not going sailing with you."

He set the basket on the table, crossed his arms over his chest and asked, "Why? Are you afraid to be alone with me?"

"I'm not afraid, Ian, just cautious," she said as she struggled to maintain her composure.

"And why do you feel the need to put your guard up, Brooke?"

Ha! He had the nerve to ask her that!

Irritation settled in her spine. "I'm not new to this game of yours, Ian."

He cast her an innocent look. "What game?"

She didn't hesitate in answering. "Your game of se-duction."

His lips quirked. "Since you think you know me so well, why are you so uptight about spending time with me? You used to know how to handle me. At least you thought you did."

A soft chuckle escaped Brooke's lips. "I didn't think anything. I did handle you. I proved that I wasn't like those half-brain tarts you used to mess around with," she said, crossing the room to him and lifting her chin.

"And furthermore, Ian Westmoreland," she added, reaching out and tapping him on the chest with her finger, "your brand of seduction won't work with me."

"And why won't it?" he asked, grabbing her finger before she jabbed a hole in his chest. "It's always worked before."

"Always worked before? Oh really, well we'll just see about that," she said over her shoulder after turning toward the bedroom. "I'll be ready in five minutes."

"Need any help getting dressed?"

"No, thank you. And if I remember correctly your expertise was in getting me undressed."

When she slammed the bedroom door shut, Ian couldn't help but smile. He remembered that fact, as well. It appeared that he would have to change his strategy a bit today, but eventually he'd have her right where he wanted her.

It was a beautiful day for sailing. The last time she had been on a boat was a couple of years ago when Malcolm had tried fixing her up with an old college pal of his. They had double dated on a deep-sea fishing trip. Unfortunately, she and the guy didn't hit it off, had nothing in common and she'd spent the entire two hours comparing him to Ian. Luckily for her, but unluckily for Malcolm, his date got seasick, and they had to return to shore earlier than planned.

"So what do you think?"

Ian's words intruded into her thoughts, and she glanced over at him and then wished she hadn't. He stood tall next to the railing, silhouetted against the noonday sun and looking every bit a sexy ship's captain. She dismissed that image from her mind and tried concentrating on the sailboat instead. According to Ian, the boat was owned by the casino, which in essence meant it was his. "This boat is a beauty, Ian."

He had surprised her by how expertly he handled the boat and all the sleek maneuvers as it glided across the waters of Lake Tahoe with ease. Whether Brooke wanted to admit it or not, it was the perfect day for an afternoon sail, and so far Ian had been the most gracious host in addition to being a well-behaved gentleman. The latter really surprised her.

The food had been delicious yet simple: ham and cheese sandwiches, chips, wine and cheesecake. Nothing fancy, nothing meant to impress. And because it shouldn't have, it did anyway. Sharing lunch with him had been wonderful. He had told her how Stone and his wife had met when they'd been on a plane together bound for Montana. He also told her of his uncle's three children. The cousins had forged a family bond with their newfound Westmoreland cousins from Texas, Uncle Corey's triplets—Clint, Cole and Casey.

"You'll like Casey if you ever get the chance to meet her," he said, taking a sip of his wine. He smiled when he added, "Her brothers had just as much trouble keeping the guys away from her as we did Delaney when she was growing up."

Brooke lifted her eyes toward the sky and breathed in the fresh April air. It was a beautiful day and being out on the lake was exactly what she needed. Had she remained at the resort she would have probably spent way to much money shopping. "I bet it was hard on the three of them, already adults before finding out their father was alive and not dead as they'd thought."

Ian nodded. "Yes, Clint and Cole are handling things okay. It's harder for Casey to come around. She was close to her mother and when Casey found out her mother had lied to them all those years, it hurt."

Ian surprised Brooke by sliding closer to where she sat. "We've talked enough about my new cousins. Now it's time to play," he said, leaning toward her with a hint of mischief in his eyes. It was then she thought that maybe she'd given him credit for being well behaved and a gentleman too soon.

"What sort of game?" she asked, suddenly feeling off balance by his closeness.

"I watched you the other night."

She had an idea where this was going and decided to see if she was right. "And?"

"You were sitting at the blackjack table."

"Go on," she encouraged.

"And I noticed something about you."

"Which was?"

"You can't play worth a damn."

Brooke's eyes widened just seconds before she burst out laughing. This definitely wasn't where she'd thought the conversation was going. And he'd said it so seriously that she quickly inwardly agreed he was telling the truth. She couldn't play worth a damn, but playing blackjack wasn't anything she did on a regular basis. "You plan on giving me a few pointers?"

He surprised her by saying yes and pulling out a deck of cards. "It's the only fair thing to do," he said grinning. "I can't have you losing all your money in the casino. It might be bad for business. So pay attention, Ms. Chamberlain."

And he spent the next hour trying to make a proficient gambler out of her.

"I really had a nice time, Ian," Brooke said later that afternoon when they had returned to the casino and he walked her to her villa.

"Prove it by going to a show with me later tonight," he said, taking her hand in his as they continued to walk toward her door.

"A show?"

"Yes, Smokey Robinson opens tonight."

Brooke's eyes widened. "*The* Smokey Robinson?"

At Ian's nod, she smiled and said. "I think he was the only other man my mother loved besides my father."

"In that case, the least you can do is go and swoon in her honor?" Ian said with a grin. He knew his mother felt the same way.

"That would be the daughterly thing to do, wouldn't it?" she asked with a teasing glint in her eyes.

He chuckled. "Of course."

"All right. Then I'll go."

They stopped in front of her door. He studied her for a long moment before saying, "I'll be by to get you for the second show at ten."

"Wouldn't it be easier for me to meet you downstairs somewhere?"

He gave her a smooth grin. Not hardly, he wanted to say. If she looked anything tonight like she had the other night when she'd shown up at the lounge, the last thing he wanted was other men hitting on her. "It's no problem. I need the exercise, anyway," he said smiling.

"Okay."

When they just stood there a minute, she gave in and asked. "Would you like to come in for a minute?"

He continued to look at her, knowing if he were to go into that room with her, it wouldn't be for just a minute. Patience, he'd discovered, was the key. He hadn't stirred up any stimulating memories like he'd originally planned to do today, but he had enjoyed the time they had spent together. And there would be other times, other opportunities. He would make sure of it.

"No, there're a couple of things I need to do before tonight," he said, stepping back. "But I dare you to ask me that same question after the show," he said, his expression suddenly turning seductive.

She grinned up at him and he knew she was taunting him when she said, "Um, I'll think about it."

He chuckled. "Yeah, you do that." And then he turned and walked away.

When Smokey sings...
The room was packed. People were even crowded around the wraparound bar in the back. But everyone's attention was on the man who'd taken center stage and was belting out "The Tracks of My Tears." His high tenor was his calling card, and the lyrics had meaning. They filled the room with love and romance.

He then did a medley of his Motown tunes and when he began singing "Oh Baby Baby," Brooke's gaze shifted to Ian. She found him staring back at her. Was he thinking the same thing she was? That in the relationship they'd once shared they had both made mistakes, or did he still blame her for everything?

She was so deep in thought that she was startled when everyone stood, began clapping and gave Smokey Robinson the standing ovation he deserved. Moments later he went into his final number, "Going to a Go-Go," and the place came alive. Older couples, who remembered the song and the dances of that day and time, got on the floor and began gyrating their bodies in all kinds of ways. Brooke couldn't help remembering her mom doing those same dances around the house when Brooke was a little girl.

"You want to go out there and try it?" Ian asked, leaning over to her. When he evidently saw the hesitancy in her eyes, he chuckled and asked, "Hey, what do we have to lose?"

She glanced at the crowd dancing and then back at him. "Parts of our face if we got in the way. They're doing a dance called 'the jerk' and I'd hate to be the recipient of one of their elbows."

Ian laughed, and although it could barely be heard above the loud music, Brooke felt the richness in the sound and was suddenly hit with a bit of nostalgia, of other times they had gone out on the town together, dancing, partying, having fun. If anyone had told her a couple of days ago that the two of them would be able to put their anger, hurt and resentment on hold for an evening, she would not have believed them. The pain had been too deep on both sides.

He leaned forward again and took her hand in his. "Come on. Let's show these old folks how to really get down."

The next thing Brooke knew they were out on the dance floor, shaking their bodies like everyone else. Ian had complimented her earlier on her choice of attire, a short, chocolate-brown silk chiffon dress with a swirling, handkerchief hemline. It gave her all the ease she needed as she moved to the music.

She couldn't recall the last time she'd gone dancing, let herself go, allowed herself a moment to feel free. Only with Ian could she be this way. Only with him.

When the music came to an end, he pulled her closer to him, lowered his head, keeping their mouths separated by a mere inch and said, "Come with me for a moment. I want to show you something."

She knew she should ask what he wanted to show her, and just where he was taking her when he led her out of the lounge. But she didn't. She couldn't. The only thing she could do was walk by his side as they held hands and pray wherever they were going, that she would still be in control when they got there.

Brooke tried not to feel nervous as they rode up in Ian's private elevator. He was leaning on the opposite wall and looking positively delicious in one of his designer suits. He stared at her and sent a torrent of sensations all through her body. The man could make everything inside of her flutter with those dark eyes of his, and she was doing everything within her might not to succumb.

"So where are you taking me?" she asked after they passed the floors to his penthouse.

He smiled before pushing off the wall. "Be patient. We'll get there soon enough."

That's what had her worried. "And just where is

'there'?" The elevator was still moving up and although she knew they were on his private side of the casino, she had no idea of where they were going. Already they had gone beyond the eighteenth floor.

Before he could open his mouth to respond—not that he would have anyway—the elevator came to a stop. She hated admitting it but he had aroused her curiosity. He had also aroused something else. Being confined in an elevator with Ian wasn't a good idea and it was taking a supreme effort on her part to downplay his sexiness. His charisma was touching her in all kinds of places, causing her body to feel hot. What she needed was a splash of cold water. The elevator door opened and she turned to follow him when he stepped out.

Her breath caught. Ian had brought her to his private conservatory. From up here, she could see everything. It was a beautiful April night, and when she glanced up she saw the sky was a beautiful shade of navy-blue. The stars sparkled like glistening diamonds above and the half moon provided a warm glow and a feeling of opulence.

Ian's conservatory was the ideal place to create a snug and relaxing haven while surrounded by the beauty of God's universe. The lighting inside the conservatory created pools of soft illumination. It was an intimate atmosphere that used the moon and stars to the best advantage. The room was furnished with several pieces of rattan furniture. Each piece was richly detailed, intricately designed out of woven banana leaf with a natural wash finish. The puffy cushions on the sofa and chair looked too comfortable for words, and the other accessories—the coffee table, side table and foot stool, added a dramatic finishing touch to the decor. Everything in the room seemed to fit. Even the tall, handsome man standing beside her.

"So what do you think?" he asked, breaking into her thoughts.

To say she was impressed was an understatement. He never ceased to amaze or surprise her. But then, she really should not have been surprised. She'd known that Ian was a very smart man who'd graduated from Yale University, magnum cum laude, at twenty-two with a degree in physics. But he definitely wasn't your ordinary geek. After working for a year at NASA's Goddard Space Flight Center, he had returned home when his grandfather died. Wanting to be close to his family he began working for a research firm in Atlanta and it was there that the gambling bug hit him. The way Ian saw it, beating the odds was based on scientific probability. To him it was a matter of science rather than a game of chance. Fortunately, he was very good at science.

"I think this place is beautiful, Ian. And the furniture and live plants enhance everything. There's nothing like having a comfortable environment with the outside all around and the sky up above."

Ian nodded. That's exactly the way he felt. He'd always loved watching the sky at night, and when he got older it had seemed the most natural thing to choose a career studying it. Although he no longer worked in that profession, he hadn't given up his love of astronomy.

"Come look through this," he said, taking her hand and leading her over to a huge, mounted telescope.

Brooke peered through the telescope at the moon, the stars and the other cool celestial objects that were now visible in the sky. She smiled when she saw a shooting star. According to myth, shooting stars fell to the earth creating a flower with each impact.

She straightened, suddenly feeling Ian's heat, and knew he had come to stand directly behind her, so close she could feel the warmth of his breath on her neck. A long, tense moment passed before she could draw in enough air to ask, "You come here often?"

"Whenever I need to get away or just to think."

Ian knew he would never tell her that although this was the first time she had been in his conservatory, he thought of her often when he was up here. It was the only place he allowed himself to let the memories of the love they'd once shared slip through the tough exterior he had built around his heart.

At one time she had been his own special star. She had shone brightly even when the skies had been gray for him and menacing dark clouds had appeared on his horizon. Brooke had been his sun after every storm.

His career change from scientist to casino owner hadn't been easy, but she, along with his family, had motivated and encouraged him to pursue his dream. Brooke had been there by his side when he had celebrated the purchase of the *Delta Princess*.

He sighed deeply, knowing two things for sure. Brooke was still deeply embedded in his system, and no matter what it took he was going to get her out of it. Just the thought of having her in his bed one last time sent a wave of heat coursing through him. But it wouldn't be fair to rush her into a night of hot, wild passion, even though that might be what they both needed.

He had to be patient.

* * *

Brooke pointed up toward the sky, trying to deflect the sensations she felt flowing through her body as a result of Ian's closeness. "Look at that star," she said.

Ian grinned and wrapped his arms around her waist, pulling her body closer to his, and whispered, "I hate to disappoint you, but that's a satellite."

"Oh." Her heart jumped, and heat suddenly flooded her spine where his chest was pressing against it. Then there was the feel of her backside pressed against the zipper of his pants. She felt the firmness of his arousal, getting thicker by the minute, and wished there was some way to defuse the tension steadily growing between them. Of course she knew that Ian would have his own ideas of how they should go about rectifying the problem.

Deciding she couldn't take much more of what she realized was his sly attempt to seduce her, Brooke turned around to suggest they go back to the lounge. Her move was a huge mistake. Turning around placed her face-to-face and body-to-body with him. When she gazed up into his eyes, she suddenly had a memory lapse, and every coherent thought froze in her brain. At that moment nothing mattered but the man staring down at her.

He reached out and traced the pad of his thumb across her jaw, and when he did, currents of electricity shot to every part of her. He leaned down and brought his face closer to hers. Up this close, underneath the beauty of a moonlit, star-glazed sky, her gaze swept over his features and her heart reaffirmed her love for him.

"Do you know what it means when a couple kisses beneath a shooting star?" he asked, his voice low and husky.

"No, what does it mean?" she asked.

"According to Greek mythology, Zeus bestows upon the couple the gift of uncontrollable passion."

Uncontrollable passion? Brooke swallowed deeply, thinking they must have kissed beneath a shooting star once before because whenever it came to passion it seemed they'd cornered the market. Back in the old days, he had been able to draw her to him with a magnetic force. Her hormones would go haywire each and every time. She felt her bones melting just thinking about those times.

"In that case I suggest we don't kiss under a shooting star," she said, trying to get a grip on her senses.

"I disagree." He moved his thumb from her jaw to her neck. "Nothing's wrong with a hefty amount of passion every once in a while," he said, leaning closer to her.

Not if you haven't had any in four years, she wanted to say, but the only thing she could do was stand and watch his mouth get closer and closer and…

Her eyes drifted shut when his lips touched hers, and when he deepened the kiss she thought there was nothing like being kissed under the beauty of a night sky, especially when the person doing the honors was the man you loved.

Brooke's insides sizzled as Ian's tongue gently, un-hurriedly mated with hers. Kissing was something she'd always enjoyed doing with him and she couldn't help but recall how they had even gone so far as to develop their own technique of French kissing. And the way Ian was using his tongue on her now jarred her senses, melting her insides. She felt heat spread up her thighs, settle between her legs, and she felt the first sign of that special brand of titillation only he could stir within her. When it came to passion, they didn't need a shooting star. Their fiery chemistry came naturally.

The room felt like it was beginning to spin when he intensified the kiss, delved deeper into her mouth, making the taste of him explode against her palate. She grabbed ahold of his shoulders, felt the material of his jacket beneath her fingers, holding on tight lest she be swept away.

When Ian finally released her mouth she could barely breathe, and a moan slipped from between her lips although she fought to hold it back. She felt the solid length of him cradled against her middle and knew what his body wanted. She tilted her head and looked at him, gazed into those dark eyes that could make a woman swoon. She was getting in deeper by the minute.

He continued to stroke the fire within her as he slid his hand up her arms, over her shoulders and leaned closer to place butterfly kisses around her nose and mouth. "I need to leave town for a few days," he said softly against her lips.

She felt her jaw go slack. "What?"

He pulled back just a little, enough for her to see the darkness of his eyes. "I need to leave in the morning for Memphis to finalize the sale of the riverboat. I'll be gone for two days."

"Oh." She tried hiding her disappointment and couldn't. Her pouty expression must have given her away.

He looked somewhat amused when he asked, "Are you going to miss me?"

She gave him a weak smile. Oh, yes, she would miss

him, but then the separation would give her a chance to screw her head back on straight. "Not at all," she said teasingly.

"Um, then maybe I should give you a reason to miss me…and to look forward to my return."

Before Brooke could draw her next breath she was swept off her feet into Ian's strong arms.

Five

Ian didn't have to go far to the sofa, which was a good thing because he was so terribly aroused his zipper was about to burst. Only Brooke could do this to him this quick and fast, with an urgency that made him want to tear the clothes off her body and do it then and there.

But he knew with Brooke he could never just do *it*. Oh, yeah, in the past they would mate like rabbits several times over, and he would take her in every position known to man—even some he'd conjured up that actually defied the laws of gravity—but still, in his mind they had never just done it. Each time they'd come together, intimately connected, it had meant something emotionally, too. They had always made love and never just had sex. Even now when he wanted to work her out of his system, he knew it would mean something.

And that was the gist of his dilemma.

Although he wanted to believe otherwise, making love to Brooke would be more than a means to an end. His best-laid intentions could backfire, and she could get even deeper under his skin. That thought was unnerving.

And yet that possibility hadn't lessened his desire for her, hadn't stopped his testosterone from kicking into overdrive or from giving him the most intense arousal he'd had in four years. In other words, he needed to "do it," like, yesterday, but only with this woman.

He leaned back on the sofa with her in his arms, and before she could open her mouth to utter a single word, his tongue was there, lapping her next breath from her parted lips. He kissed her deeply. His heart throbbed, his pulse was going haywire and his hands seemed to be everywhere, but mostly working their way under her dress.

When he realized that in less than five seconds flat he had his fingers right smack between her legs, he snapped his head up and stared at her. This was madness. This was crazy. This was typical Ian and Brooke.

He drew in an unsteady breath when these thoughts rang through his mind. They had always been hot for each other, and nothing had changed. Together they were spontaneous as hell. Whenever their bodies joined as one all they had to do was think orgasm and it happened.

He saw the darkening of her eyes, a signal that she wanted him as much as he wanted her. But he needed to hear her say it. He had to know before he went any further that whatever they did tonight, she would be with him all the way and there would be no regrets.

"Brooke?"

* * *

She heard her name whispered from his lips in a tone so raspy and sensual it made her breath hitch in her throat. She knew what he wanted. She also knew what he was asking, and at the moment she couldn't deny Ian Westmoreland a single thing. It had been four years for her, and the abstinence had taken its toll. She felt out of her league, something she'd never felt with Ian before. She didn't know how to react. The only thing she did know was that she wanted him.

She reached out and clutched the lapels of his jacket. "I don't understand the intensity of this, Ian," she whispered truthfully, pulling his mouth down closer to hers.

"Then let me explain it to you without words," he said silkily against her lips.

And then he was kissing her again, and with their mouths still connected he slid to the edge of the sofa. Shifting her in his arms he changed her position in his lap and brought her legs around his waist. With her dress bunched up around her waist, she felt the thickness of his arousal pressed against the juncture of her legs. There was no way she could regain her senses now even if she wanted to. She was a goner.

Heat flared through her when she felt the straps of her dress fall from her shoulders, and then he was no longer kissing her. He had turned his attention to her breasts. Being braless left her bare and exposed for his pleasure, and when his mouth latched on to a nipple she knew this was just the beginning. When it came to breast stimulation he was as skilled as they came.

"Ian."

Ian pulled away, deciding he would take more time

with her breasts later. He knew exactly what they both wanted and needed now. He stood with her in his arms when the ring of his cell phone intruded.

"Damn," he muttered as he placed her on her feet while working the phone out of his jacket. "What?" he barked after answering the call.

"Domestic dispute," Vance said, the security manager's words washing over Ian like a pail of cold water. "One of those electricians got a surprise visit from his wife."

"And?"

"She caught him in bed with…" After a brief pause Vance added, "…another electrician. Male."

"What?"

"You heard me right. And now the woman is hysterical."

Ian rubbed his hand down his face. He couldn't very much blame her for that. Because of the satellite floating overhead, the reception was clear, and standing close in front of him he knew that Brooke had heard Vance's words. Ian met her gaze and, regardless of the situation, he was tempted to sweep his mouth down for another tongue-tingling kiss. Instead he said to Vance, "Go on, I'm sure there's more."

"Yes. She's threatened to sue everyone—the electricians' union, the airline that flew him here, the guy he was caught with, as well as this casino for allowing such behavior and conduct."

Ian didn't like hearing the word *sue.* "Where are you?"

"On the fourteenth floor."

"I'm on my way." He flipped the phone shut and gazed into Brooke's face thinking how damn sexy she looked with her hair mussed and her lips swollen from his kisses.

"I need to go," he said regretfully, straightening his jacket.

"I understand how it is when duty calls."

A small smile tugged at his lips. "I appreciate that." Straightening out the situation might take a while, and since it was almost two in the morning, Ian knew it would be two days before he saw Brooke again.

He took her hand in his as he led her toward the elevator. "Enjoy yourself while I'm in Memphis."

She smiled over at him. "I will."

He frowned. "But not too much."

She chuckled. "Okay, I won't."

When the elevator closed behind them, he pulled her into his arms. He thought of asking her to come to Memphis with him but quickly pushed the idea from his mind. Instead he said, "Have dinner with me in my penthouse when I get back."

He thought it was better to ask now. He had a feeling the two-day separation would have her thinking that tonight had been a mistake, and he didn't intend to let that happen.

"Ian, I—"

He kissed the words off her lips. "No, Brooke. We owe it to ourselves to finish what we started."

She stared up at him. "Do we?"

"Yes." And then he kissed her again, liking the feel of her in his arms, her warmth, her closeness and definitely her taste.

When he released her mouth she sighed deeply and said, "All right."

Tension that had been building inside of him slowly left his body. "I'll see you to your suite."

She shook her head. "That's not necessary, Ian. You have a matter that needs your immediate attention. Besides," she said, smiling, "I think I'll stop at one of the blackjack tables and try out some of those skills you taught me today."

He chuckled. "Okay."

"Have a safe trip, Ian."

"Thank you."

As the elevator arrived on the lobby floor, he released her. When she stepped away he suddenly felt a rush of loss through every part of his body. And when she began walking off he called out to her before she was swallowed by the crowd. "Don't forget about dinner Friday night."

She turned around and smiled. "I won't."

"My place. Seven sharp."

She nodded and continued to stare at him until the elevator door closed.

Brooke sat idly at a table in one of the cafés sipping her coffee and thinking of her telephone conversation with Tara Westmoreland that morning. Tara was Delaney's best friend and was married to Delaney's brother Thorn Westmoreland. Tara had invited Brooke to the surprise thirtieth birthday party being planned for Delaney next weekend at the Rolling Cascade.

Brooke was surprised Ian hadn't mentioned anything about the party to her. Perhaps he didn't want her there. She could remember how tense things had been at Dare and Shelly's wedding. But at that time the relationship between her and Ian had been very strained. Now, although they weren't back together or anything like that, at least they were talking…and kissing, she thought, smiling to herself. However, he might not want to give his family the wrong impression, and if they were seen together she could certainly see that happening.

"Enjoying your stay, Ms. Chamberlain?"

Brooke glanced up and met Vance's less-than-friendly eyes. On more than one occasion she had caught the man staring at her as if he was deliberately keeping her within his scope, and more than once she had wondered if Ian had asked him to keep an eye on her while he was gone. If he had, that meant he suspected her of something. It also meant he still didn't trust her.

Her heart quickened and she inwardly scolded herself for jumping to conclusions. This man was head of security at the casino and he was probably programmed to be suspicious of everything and everyone.

"Yes, I'm enjoying myself. This is a beautiful casino."

"I think so, too."

"And please, call me Brooke."

"Okay, and I'm Vance."

Brooke nodded. She was very much aware of who he was. He was the man who had taken her to Ian's office that first day. She had a feeling that had she refused he would have found a way to get her up there anyway with minimum fuss. He had that air about him, a no-nonsense, get-the-job-done sort of guy, and she wondered if he'd had a history at some point with the Bureau.

"Would you like to join me for coffee, Vance?" she asked, nodding to the huge coffeepot sitting in the middle of the table.

He surprised her when he said, "Don't mind if I do." And then he took the seat across from her. She leaned back in her chair. He had asked his question and now it was time to ask hers. He was former military; that was a given from his demeanor. But she needed to know something else about him.

"What Special Forces or federal agency were you affiliated with, Vance?"

His blue eyes, sharp and clear, riveted to hers as he poured a cup of coffee. "What makes you think I was part of the military or an agency?"

She shrugged. "Your mannerisms."

He chuckled. "I guess it takes one to know one."

She raised her brow, and before she could say anything, he said, "Don't bother denying it. Ian told me. Only because he knew he could trust me. So your secret's safe."

She took a sip of her own coffee and then said, "It's not a secret. It's just that my profession isn't anybody's business."

He moved his massive shoulders in a shrug. "Like I said, Ian mentioned it. As head of security here he felt I should know."

She nodded and wondered what else Ian might have told him. "You still haven't answered my question," she decided to remind him.

"I didn't, did I," he said, smiling coyly. "I was in the Corp and then I worked for the Bureau awhile before taking a position in the Secret Service."

The executive branch, Brooke mused. "I take it you know Quade," she said of Ian's twin brother.

Vance grinned fondly. "Yes, I know Quade. In fact I'm the one who trained him for his first assignment. Quade and I worked together for years and that's how I met Ian. When I decided to retire after twenty-five years in the service, Quade knew I wasn't one to sit idle and twiddle my thumbs. He mentioned Ian had a position here that I might be interested in. The rest, as they say, is history."

Brooke smiled. "And from what I can see, the way you run things indicates you're the right man for the job," she said honestly.

"Thanks."

She seriously meant the compliment. Her eyes and ears had been open and she'd seen how he had expertly and professionally, with the authority that could only come from someone with his years of experience, handled several potentially troublesome incidents.

"If I didn't know better I'd think you were a member of my staff, Brooke."

Brooke met his gaze over the rim of her cup after catching his meaning. He was no rookie and although she had tried to be discreet in her inquiries, he had been alert and had picked up on her interests. "Part of the job."

"Yes, but you're not working, are you? At least, that's what Ian told me. He said you were here for rest and relaxation."

She placed her cup down and straightened in her seat, deciding this wily old fox missed nothing. "Ian was right. What I meant when I said part of the job was that after a while, once you've been an agent, certain things become second nature."

"Oh, like being observant and noticing every little thing?"

"Yes, like being observant and noticing every little thing." She couldn't help but wonder if he believed her.

She watched as he leaned forward and then he said,

"I guess a second pair of eyes never hurt. But I think we need to clear the air about something. Ian is a good man. Although he's a lot younger than most casino owners, he has a good sense for business. Somehow with that scientific mind of his he has the ability to play the odds and come up a winner. This place is a testimony to that. Investors trust him with their money because he has a proven track record of running a clean, profitable operation. My job is to be his eyes and ears as well as to protect his back. And, more important, Ian is not just my boss, I consider him a good friend."

Brooke picked up her coffee cup and stared down into the dark liquid a moment before meeting Vance's gaze and asking, "Is there a reason you're telling me this?"

He chuckled softly. "Only you can answer that, Brooke."

She held Vance's gaze. "No matter what you or anyone else might think, I trust Ian implicitly."

"But…"

"But I think we should end this conversation," Brooke said frowning, thinking she might have said too much already. Vance was no fool. He was as sharp as they came, and with his history he probably knew she had lied through her teeth when she claimed she was at the casino for rest and relaxation.

Vance laughed, breaking into her thoughts. "You're good, Brooke, and because I like you, I'm going to show you just how good an operation Ian runs," he said as he stood. "How about coming with me."

Two hours later Brooke had returned to her room to rest up a bit before changing for dinner. Vance had given her a tour of the casino's security surveillance center upstairs, and she'd had to agree with him that not too much went on in the casino that he wasn't aware of, including the lovers tryst between those electricians. Although there weren't any video cameras in individual rooms, they were installed in the elevators, hallways, lobby and every other inch of the casino. Security had noticed the excessive amount of time the two men had been visiting each other's rooms during the late-night hours.

Vance had also told her that being the born diplomat Ian was, he had brought a semblance of order to the situation last night, although there was only so much one could do after a woman discovered her husband had been unfaithful, and with someone of the same sex.

Brooke was just about to walk into the bathroom to run her shower when the phone rang. She quickly crossed the room to pick it up. "Hello."

"Miss me yet?"

Although Ian's voice sounded cool and in control, Brooke felt shivers tingle up her spine, anyway. His call had definitely caught her off guard. He had to have been thinking about her to have called. The mere fact that he had brought a smile to her lips. "No, I've been too busy to miss you," she said teasingly.

"Oh, and what have you been doing?"

Brooke glanced out of the window. The view of the mountains was breathtaking, but the mountains weren't the main thing on her mind now. The man she was talking to was.

She thought back to his question, doubting he would appreciate knowing Vance had given her a tour of his security setup. "I've been doing a lot of things but mostly perfecting my blackjack skills."

His laugh sent a warm feeling all through her stomach. "I hope you won't be breaking the casino before I return."

"I'll try not to, but I have been lucky a few times."

"Luck has nothing to do with it. Like I've told you, it's merely a matter of science."

"If you say so. Will you still be returning tomorrow night?"

"Those are my plans and so far things are running on schedule. I should be able to wrap up in the morning and arrive there by late afternoon."

Brooke nodded. She didn't want to admit it but she *had* missed him. The mere fact that until this week she hadn't seen him in four years meant nothing. Once she'd seen him her heart had remembered; unfortunately, so had her body.

"What are your plans for the rest of the day?"

His question pulled in her thoughts. "To shop until I drop." She then decided to mention something that had been bothering her all day. "I got a call from Tara this morning inviting me to Delaney's surprise birthday party. Why didn't you mention it?"

"I really didn't think about it much. Besides, I figured sooner or later you would hear from some member of my family."

"And how do you feel about me being there?" she questioned.

"Why are you asking me that? Is there a certain way I should feel, Brooke?"

"I don't know," she replied quietly. "I know how tense I made you feel being at Dare's wedding."

"At the time, considering everything, I think a certain degree of discomfort for both of us was understandable."

"And now?"

"Now I think we're a lot more at ease with each other, don't you?"

Considering how they'd been spending a lot of their time while they'd been together she would definitely say yes. "I just don't want you to get bent all out of shape if your family starts assuming things about us."

"I'm used to my family, Brooke. Maybe the real question is whether or not you'll get bent out of shape. My mom refuses to believe that you and I won't ever work out our problems and get back together, no matter what I've told her to the contrary. She likes you. Always has."

Brooke smiled. She'd always liked his mom, as well.

"So are you thinking about going?"

"Probably," she replied, hoping that making an appearance wouldn't cause a big commotion. Unfortunately, there didn't seem to be any way to avoid it. Everyone had known how serious her and Ian's relationship was at one time, and she was sure some of them didn't know the reason for their breakup. Although he was close to his family, Ian was a private person when it came to his personal life.

"And you're sure you won't have a problem if I decide to go?" she asked again.

"Yes, I'm sure I won't have a problem with it." He chuckled. "Besides, it's about time I give the family something to talk about. Things have been pretty quiet since Durango got married a few months ago, and I'll be the first to admit that we Westmorelands need a little craziness every once in a while."

* * *

A half hour later Ian sat and reflected on his conversation with Brooke. He'd asked her if she'd missed him and before they'd hung up he'd gotten her to admit she had. That meant he was making progress. But the truth was that he wasn't faring much better. He missed her, too.

He should never have let her back into his life, but now that she was, he was in a bad way. It was crazy what mere kisses could do to a man.

It had been more than just the kisses, though. It had been her presence and the heated attraction that enveloped them each and every time they were together.

"Would you like anything else to drink, sir?"

Ian glanced up at the waiter. He had dined alone at a restaurant known for its sizzling and delicious steaks. The food had been excellent, but the only sizzling and delicious thing on his mind during the entire meal had been Brooke.

"No, that will be all for now."

What Ian wanted was a quiet moment to just sit, sip his wine and pine for the woman he desired more than anything else. He longed to see her again, take her into his arms, make love to her on his bed or hers—which technically was also his because he owned the casino—and take her to a place he hadn't been since they'd separated. A place that had his insides coiling just thinking about it. It had been a place they'd discovered years ago; it had been their own universe, their own solar system, a personal space only the two of them occupied.

The hand holding his wineglass tightened as he felt that same squeeze in his groin. How could one woman stir up his passion, his desire and his lust to such unprecedented proportions?

"Ian?"

Snatched from his heated musings, Ian glanced up at the very attractive woman standing beside his table. He smiled at her. "Casey, what are you doing here in Memphis?" he asked his cousin as he came to his feet. The last time he'd seen her was at his brother Durango's wedding reception in Atlanta.

"I'm on a buying trip for my store," she said smiling back at him. "I'll be here for a couple of days. What about you?"

"I'm here on business and I'll flying out in the morning." Ian knew she owned a fashion boutique back in Beaumont, Texas. "Come join me," he invited, pulling out a chair for her. "Would you like to order something?" he asked, not sure if she'd eaten yet.

"Thanks," she said as she sat down. "But, no. I've just finished eating and was about to leave. I thought it was you from across the room, but I wasn't sure, and for a moment I was hesitant about coming over to ask. You seemed deeply absorbed in thought."

He sat back down and chuckled. "I was," he said without any further explanation. It was best she didn't know what he'd been thinking about. "So are you coming to Delaney's surprise party next week at the casino?"

He saw her grimace slightly and knew she hadn't yet made up her mind. Whereas her brothers Clint and Cole had quickly meshed into the Westmoreland family fold, Casey was still a little reserved. Evidently after thinking for years that her family consisted of only her and her two brothers, the multitude of Westmorelands overwhelmed her.

"Do you know if my father is coming?" she asked.

"Yes, as far as I know Uncle Corey's coming," Ian said, taking another sip of his drink. "I can't see him missing it."

He knew Casey was still struggling to develop a relationship with the father she hadn't known she had. All those years she'd thought he was dead.

"I'm thinking about taking him up on his offer and spending a month in Montana," Casey said.

Ian raised a brow. He'd heard his uncle making the invitation, but Ian hadn't been sure Casey would accept it. For her to be considering the visit was a huge step in building a relationship with her father.

"I think that's a wonderful idea, Casey," Ian said. "And I'm sure Uncle Corey and Abby would love having you spend some time with them."

While kicking back and enjoying the taste of his wine, Ian listened as Casey brought him up to date on her brothers, who were both Texas Rangers. She knew for certain they would be at Delaney's party, but Ian noticed she still hadn't answered his question as to whether or not she would make an appearance.

An hour or so later, Ian opened the door to his hotel room. He glanced across the room. His bags were all packed and he was ready to go. Hell, he would leave tonight if he could get a flight out. To say he was eager to return to Lake Tahoe was an understatement.

Even now he wanted to pick up the phone and call Brooke but he kept reminding himself he had spoken to her earlier. He shook his head as he began undressing, wondering what in the hell was happening to him. Brooke walks back into his life and his mind goes bonkers. Okay, she was the sexiest thing he'd ever laid eyes on, both then and now, but still, that wasn't a good enough reason to get carried away.

But he *was* getting carried away. He was beginning to feel emotions that he hadn't felt in years. He raked his hand over his head thinking that wasn't a good thing, but for now there wasn't anything he could do about it.

Not a damn thing.

Six

Brooke had spent the past two days shopping and enjoying a lot of the amenities the resort had to offer and, of course, keeping her eyes and ears open while doing so. Now the day Ian was scheduled to return had arrived, and as she lowered her body into the warm water of the Jacuzzi tub in her bathroom, excitement filled her to a degree she hadn't known in a long time. She submerged her body deep into the tub and let the jets provide a deep massage for the muscles she had overworked during her two-day shopping spree.

She laid her head back and closed her eyes as the jets and the bubbles whisked her away to another place, tantalizing as well as soothing her state of mind, sharpening her focus and her outlook.

Another moan escaped her lips when she shifted her body and doing so shot a jet of water to the area between her legs. She smiled thinking that was some kind of massage therapy. But she was realistic enough to know that the only way the deep-rooted tension and urgency that had settled in that part of her body could be removed was by the skill of one man.

Ian Westmoreland.

As her eyes remained closed she contemplated how their dinner that evening would go. She could remember sharing meals with him at other times and how things ended. The memories sent shivers all through her body. He hadn't earned the nickname the Perfect End for nothing.

A couple of hours later, after her bath and a short nap, Brooke began getting dressed. Although she didn't agree that one more time between the sheets would get them out of each other's systems, she did agree that they needed one last time together to put an ending chapter to what once had been a beautiful relationship.

The thought of finality tightened the muscles surrounding her heart but she knew it had to be. She had to finally move forward in her life. She was young and believed that sooner or later she would get over Ian, no matter how hard such a thing would be. When she returned to D.C. she would ask Malcolm for a couple of weeks off.

She needed time alone to sort things out and to put her life in order. She also needed to make some decisions regarding her future. If she decided to leave fieldwork, she needed to know what other opportunities the Bureau had to offer. When she had mentioned such a possibility to Vance, he had suggested a job at the White House. Apparently, there were always places for capable women on the first lady's security detail.

A smile touched her lips when she thought of the time she'd spent with Vance. In the end, she'd decided that she liked him because he had Ian's best interest at heart and he was loyal to those he cared about. Ian was like that, too. Ian's sense of loyalty was the main reason he couldn't get past the Boris Knowles case.

She glanced at the underthings she had placed on her bed, items she had purchased that day. Ian always loved black lace on her, and she was going to make sure that tonight he saw a lot of it.

She squared her shoulders after dabbing perfume on her pulse points and between her breasts. The outfit she had bought to wear was an attention getter. It was meant to tease, tantalize, to impress and undress all in one sweep. She intended to make their last time together special.

Tonight she would be the one to give them the perfect end.

It felt good being back, Ian thought, as he walked into the penthouse a little later than he'd wanted. His connecting flight had been hell, with enough turbulence to make even a grown man weep.

The first thing he'd wanted to do when he had arrived at the casino was to find Brooke, but Vance had mentioned he had seen her leave the resort earlier. She had been headed for the shops in town. It had looked as if she intended to do some serious shopping. Ian had ended up going to his penthouse a disenchanted man. He unpacked with the thought that he was preparing for a night he intended Brooke would remember for a long time.

Ian checked his watch a few hours later. It was ten to seven. Where was she? He distinctively remembered

Brooke always showed up at any destination a few minutes earlier than scheduled. Of all the nights for her to change her routine and—

His breath caught when he heard the ringing of his elevator alerting him he was about to have a visitor. Deciding this would be a special night, he had changed into a pair of black trousers and a white button-up shirt. But to give his outfit a casual spin he had left his shoes off. He wanted to look totally at home, totally relaxed and completely in control.

He walked over to the elevator and was standing there when it opened. As soon as it did, his throat suddenly felt tight and he could only stare, almost tongue-tied as he feasted his eyes on Brooke. She was wearing a short, lacy black concoction that seemed to scream, strip me. His fingertips began to itch, wanting to do that very thing.

"I know I'm early, but aren't you going to invite me in?"

Hell, he planned to do better than that, he thought, edging backward so she could take a step forward. When she did, the elevator door swooshed close. "Welcome back, Ian."

God, he'd missed her. In just a couple of days she had gotten back under his skin. Deep. He opened his mouth to reply but no sound came out. His mind couldn't get beyond the fact that she was standing there wearing black lace. She of all people knew how he felt about black lace; especially on her. She could wear it like no other woman. He was aroused to the nth degree from just seeing her in it.

The itching in his fingers intensified and a need he tried to ignore gripped him, made his blood sizzle and his heart pound in his chest. He took a step forward. It was then that he studied her face; a face that had invaded his dreams so many times over the past four years; a face he couldn't forget no matter how he tried.

Ian quickly accepted the fact that it wasn't about the dress Brooke was wearing or how sexy she looked in it that made him so attracted to her. Brooke, the unique individual she'd always been, had captured his interest from the first and still held it tight.

But still…he had to give kudos to the dress. It made a provocative statement, and seeing her in it did the things to him she'd known it would.

"Ian?"

His gaze returned to her face. He watched her mouth quiver and decided to kiss that quiver right off her lips. He intended to give her a proper hello, Ian Westmoreland style. Leaning over, he ran his fingertips along her jaw and then, leaning closer still, he began gently nibbling on her lips, savoring the moment and relishing the sweet taste of her and the feel of her full lips beneath his.

He had wanted to linger, but the need hammering inside of him wouldn't let him. It drove an urgency he couldn't control, and when her moan filled his mouth he indulged her by taking the kiss deeper. All the long-denied needs he'd pretended weren't there were hitting him full force, begging for the kind of release only she could give.

He tightened his hold on her as his mouth mated with hers, slowly yet torridly, taking his breath away with every return stroke of her tongue while it moved sensuously in his mouth, hitting those spots she knew from the past could drive him mad with desire.

One thing he and Brooke had enjoyed doing as a

An Important Message from the Editors

Dear Reader,

Because you've chosen to read one of our fine romance novels, we'd like to say "thank you!" And, as a **special** way to thank you, we've selected <u>two more</u> of the books you love so well **plus** two exciting Mystery Gifts to send you — absolutely <u>FREE</u>!

Please enjoy them with our compliments...

Pam Powers

Lift here

Peel off seal and place inside...

How to validate your Editor's "Thank You" FREE GIFTS

1. Peel off gift seal from front cover. Place it in space provided at right. This automatically entitles you to receive 2 FREE BOOKS and 2 FREE mystery gifts.

2. Send back this card and you'll get 2 new Silhouette *Desire*® novels. These books have a cover price of $4.50 or more each in the U.S. and $5.25 or more each in Canada, but they are yours to keep absolutely free.

3. There's no catch. You're under no obligation to buy anything. We charge nothing—ZERO—for your first shipment. And you don't have to make any minimum number of purchases—not even one!

4. The fact is, thousands of readers enjoy receiving their books by mail from The Silhouette Reader Service™. They enjoy the convenience of home delivery...they like getting the best new novels at discount prices BEFORE they're available in stores...and they love their Reader to Reader subscriber newsletter featuring author news, special book offers, book reviews and much more!

5. We hope that after receiving your free books you'll want to remain a subscriber. But the choice is yours— to continue or cancel, any time at all! So why not take us up on our invitation, with no risk of any kind. You'll be glad you did!

GET TWO *Free* MYSTERY GIFTS...

SURPRISE MYSTERY GIFTS COULD BE YOURS **FREE** AS A SPECIAL "THANK YOU" FROM THE EDITORS

DETACH AND MAIL CARD TODAY!

Yes!
I have placed my Editor's "Thank You" seal in the space provided at right. Please send me 2 free books and 2 free mystery gifts. I understand I am under no obligation to purchase any books, as explained on the back and on the opposite page.

PLACE
FREE GIFTS
SEAL
HERE

326 SDL EFYF   225 SDL EFW4

FIRST NAME	LAST NAME

ADDRESS

APT.#   CITY

STATE/PROV.   ZIP/POSTAL CODE

(S-D-08/06)

Thank You!

The Silhouette Reader Service™ — Here's How It Works:

Accepting your 2 free books and 2 free mystery gifts places you under no obligation to buy anything. You may keep the books and gifts and return the shipping statement marked "cancel." If you do not cancel, about a month later we'll send you 6 additional books and bill you just $3.80 each in the U.S., or $4.47 each in Canada, plus 25¢ shipping & handling per book and applicable taxes if any.* That's the complete price and — compared to cover prices starting from $4.50 each in the U.S. and $5.25 each in Canada — it's quite a bargain! You may cancel at any time, but if you choose to continue, every month we'll send you 6 more books, which you may either purchase at the discount price or return to us and cancel your subscription.

*Terms and prices subject to change without notice. Sales tax applicable in N.Y. Canadian residents will be charged applicable provincial taxes and GST. All orders subject to approval. Credit or debit balances in a customer's account(s) may be offset by any other outstanding balance owed by or to the customer. Please allow 4 to 6 weeks for delivery.

If offer card is missing write to: The Silhouette Reader Service, 3010 Walden Ave., P.O. Box 1867, Buffalo, NY 14240-9952

BUSINESS REPLY MAIL
FIRST-CLASS MAIL   PERMIT NO. 717-003   BUFFALO, NY

POSTAGE WILL BE PAID BY ADDRESSEE

SILHOUETTE READER SERVICE
3010 WALDEN AVE
PO BOX 1867
BUFFALO NY 14240-9952

NO POSTAGE
NECESSARY
IF MAILED
IN THE
UNITED STATES

couple was exploring new things in the bedroom, and on one occasion they'd had a kiss-a-thon. By the time it was over, they had explored every kissing tip known to man and had gone further by inventing some of their own.

And she remembered, he thought, as his hands on her hips tightened and he pulled her closer to him. Not only had she remembered but she was putting some of those techniques into action, making blood pulse through his veins and sending heat spreading all through him; especially his loins. With a mastery and skill that almost made him weak in the knees, she was taking over the kiss, making him groan into her mouth and reminding him why he had fallen so hard for her years ago. Brooke had a way of taking him by surprise.

And she was doing it now.

He definitely hadn't expected this, a kiss that went far and beyond any fantasy he'd ever had. He had figured she would be reluctant, would fight the intensity of the chemistry they were feeling. But she wasn't. In her own way she was letting him know that she needed to move on with her life just as he needed to move on with his. She accepted that there could never be a reconciliation. They needed closure, and this was the only way they would get it. She was kissing him with a passion that sent shivers vibrating through his body and he was greedily lapping it up.

"Brooke," he whispered when she finally released his mouth. But before she could take a step back, he swept her into his arms and once again covered her lips with his.

She could go on kissing him forever, Brooke thought, as Ian kissed her and she greedily kissed him back with equal fervor. And moments later when he released her mouth and began walking with her in his arms, her breath caught in her chest as he moved up the stairs to his bedroom.

She glanced up, saw the smoldering look of desire in his eyes, and the pressure mounting inside her escalated.

When he came to a stop, she glanced around and he slowly placed her on her feet, sliding her body against his in the process, letting her feel the bulge in his pants, evidence of his intense desire for her.

He tipped her chin up and met her gaze. "I want you."

His words made her draw in a shaky breath. It had been four years since she had been with a man, and her body was attuned to Ian in a profound way. He was the one and only man she'd ever been intimate with. Something deep within her began to prepare her for the pleasure she knew only he could give with those wonderful hands, that skillful tongue and that big strong body. Just thinking about what was to come had sensations erupting all the way inside her womb.

"And I want you, too, Ian," she said breathlessly as she felt her center began to quake with a longing she hadn't felt in a long time. "Tonight, I need you," she added.

"Not as much as I need you," he replied, reaching out to remove her dress.

A hiss escaped between Ian's teeth when he pulled the dress over her head and tossed it aside only to reveal more black lace—a sexy bra and silky high-cut panties. Unable to help himself, he dropped to his knees right there in the middle of the room and buried his face in her belly, needing the scent of her in his nostrils and the taste of her on his tongue.

He leaned forward and began licking the hollow of her navel while easing her panties down her legs. He paused only long enough for her to step out of them before nipping at her belly and moving lower.

He pulled back for a moment and looked up at her. He continued to hold her gaze as he reached out and slipped one hand between her legs, letting his fingers go to work in her damp flesh. And when she grabbed hold of his shoulders and began moaning and grinding against his hand he knew she was on the brink of an orgasm so explosive she would have it right there if he didn't do something.

And so he did.

He broke eye contact with her and dipped his head and glided his tongue over her, into her, exploring, probing and loving her in a way he hadn't wanted to do with any other woman. His hands held tight to her thighs as his tongue continued its assault with hard, steady strokes, needing the taste of her in each and every part of his mouth.

He tasted her shivers, felt a shudder shake her body and heard her moan his name as she automatically bucked against his mouth, but he refused to pull back. Instead his tongue seemed to go into a frenzy, and it took her with a greediness that sent tremors through him.

A strangled growl escaped his lips when her spasms ended. He stood and quieted her aftershocks with his mouth on hers, needing to kiss her again. And then he was sweeping her into his arms and taking her to his bed and placing her on his satin bedspread.

He slid a hand to her chest and undid the front clasp of her bra and eased her out of it, tossing it aside. He'd always thought that her breasts were the most beautiful in the world and automatically he leaned forward and rubbed his face against them, licking the area between her breasts before latching his lips onto a hardened nipple and drawing it into his mouth.

Ignoring her moans, he suckled hard, deep, relentlessly, one then the other, once again mesmerized by her taste, and when he couldn't hold back any longer, he stood and hurriedly stripped off his clothes, needing to be joined with her with such an intense need that his entire body was throbbing. And when he came back to the bed, she reached out and her hands captured his engorged flesh as if she needed to touch it, become reacquainted with the feel of it. When she began stroking him, he almost lost it.

"Easy, baby," he murmured as his knee pressed into the mattress. "Too much of that and I'm a goner." He moved to position his body over hers and nudged her legs apart with his knee.

His gaze locked on hers. He knew she'd been taking the Pill for years to regulate her periods, but for both of their protection, he reached into a small table and retrieved a foil square.

Before he could open the small packet, Brooke took it, opened it and carefully placed the sheath on his erection.

He reached out and brushed his hand against her cheek. "I want you so much, Brooke," he murmured softly, and then with a primal growl he entered her, throwing his head back as something wild, primitive and obsessive took control inside him.

She was tight, nearly as tight as she'd been the first time they'd made love and she'd been a virgin. It wasn't his imagination, and he met her gaze, ignoring the hunger that propelled him to start moving. She was so tight that it felt like she was squeezing him, locking her feminine muscles securely around him, claiming him, making sure he couldn't pull out even if he wanted to.

She didn't have that to worry about. He wasn't going anywhere other than deeper inside her once he fully understood just what the tightness of her body meant. He met her gaze, and the look she gave him all but said, You figure it out.

So he did.

"This is the first time for you since…?" He couldn't finish the question, since the very thought shocked the hell out of him. Four years was a long time and her devotion to him was the most touching thing he could ever imagine. The very idea that even now he had been her first and only lover tore a soundless howl of possessiveness from his throat. Her body knew him and only him.

At that precise moment he wanted her with a passion he'd never felt before. Grasping her hips he began moving, stroking back and forth inside of her, going deeper. Her muscles clenched with each and every thrust he made, forcing his strokes to become more frantic.

He had to look at her, had to remember this moment for the rest of his life, and he brought his head forward, met her gaze and saw the heat in her eyes and knew neither of them could last much longer although they were fighting to do so. This would be the last time they came together this way, and they intended to make a memory to last a lifetime.

The thought, the very idea of not making love to her ever again, had him leaning forward, nipping at her shoulders, branding her while he felt her fingertips dig into his back as if to brand him, as well.

"Ian, I—"

He kissed the words off her lips. There was nothing to be said and when an explosion sent a million shudders ramming through his body, a loud growl tore from his throat through clenched teeth. He felt her come apart in his arms which caused another orgasm to rip through him. He thought he was going to die and quickly decided if he was about to take his last breath then this was definitely the way to go about it.

And he knew, as he buried himself inside of her to the hilt again as a third orgasm quickly hit him and triggered a similar explosion inside her body and he began rocking back and forth inside of her with a hunger that wouldn't let up, that he had miscalculated his emotions.

He'd erroneously figured he could sleep with her this one last time and be done with it, effectively getting her out of his system. Instead, as he cupped her buttocks tighter in his hands and felt her thighs quake beneath his at the same time his release shot deep into her womb, he knew that she had burrowed deeper into it.

"Stay here and rest. I'll let you know when dinner is ready," Ian's warm breath whispered against Brooke's ear before he slipped out of bed.

He glanced back over his shoulder long enough to see her eyes slowly drift open at the same time an adorable smile touched her lips as she snuggled under the covers. "Um, okay."

His lips twitched into a smile. He'd totally worn the woman out. She needed rest, and the only way to guarantee that she got it was for him to leave for a while. So after putting his pants back on he quietly eased open the door and slipped out of the room.

Talk about him being obsessed with making love to her. They hadn't made it past the foyer. She'd had no idea he'd set the stage for seduction with romantic lit candles. Their pure vanilla fragrance was sending a sweet scent through the rooms. He knew Brooke was partial to Thai food and so he'd had one of the resort restaurants prepare a special meal for them. He hoped the meal he had selected would please her. Making his way across the room, he picked up the phone and within minutes had instructed room service to deliver their dinner to his penthouse.

Knowing there was nothing for him to do but wait, he walked over to the window and looked out. It was dark outside, but the shape of the mountains could be seen across the lake. He would love to share this beautiful view with Brooke.

If he were to go back to his bedroom now and wake her he would do more than just show her the view. It was bad enough that he had to get her up when their meal came. He wouldn't take any chances. Brooke was too much of a temptation, and now that he had made love to her he wanted her more and more.

The memory of their bodies tangled together in his bed was so vivid in his mind that his blood was racing through his veins a little too fast to suit him. Although they had turned the heat up a notch, in fact had kicked it into a full blaze in his bed, a part of him refused to remain anything but cautious where she was concerned. She had hurt him once and could possibly do it again and he wasn't a glutton for punishment.

"Ian?"

At the sound of her soft voice he felt his entire body go tense. Squaring his shoulders and taking a deep breath, he turned around. Immediately he wished he hadn't. She was wearing the shirt he'd worn earlier, but she hadn't bothered to button it up, giving him a good frontal view.

He heard himself groan as his mind savored what he was seeing. There was nothing more beautiful than a naked or half-naked Brooke. A Brooke who'd recently been made love to or a Brooke who was wearing a let's-do-it-again look on her face.

The memories of what they had shared in his bedroom were tossing his mind every which way but loose. He fought for composure. He fought for control. He fought the urge to cross the room and take her again. If she was trying to get him all hot and bothered again, it was a complete waste of time because he was already there. He hadn't cooled down from the last time.

"Yes, Brooke?" he answered in a low, barely audible voice. "What is it that you want?"

He met her gaze. Heaven help him if she even hinted that she wanted him to make love to her again. There was no way he would be able to resist. Even now his arousal was thickening beneath his zipper. "Just tell me what you want, sweetheart. Your every wish is my command."

Brooke's breath caught as Ian's gaze held hers. She tried to remember the last time he had called her sweetheart and couldn't, it had seemed so long ago. But the endearment had flowed off his lips just as easily as it used to. And then there was the way he was looking at her with dark eyes filled with more than just heat and desire. Hope escalated within her at the thought that maybe, possibly…

She quickly pushed the far-fetched thought from her mind. Ian might desire her but he no longer loved her. She tried to think but decided she couldn't think very well with him looking at her like that. He'd said her every wish was his command. Well, she decided to put him to the test.

"How soon will the food arrive?" she asked, sliding into one of the high-back chairs at the casino-style blackjack table in the room.

"How soon do you want it?"

She smiled, wondering if they were still talking about the food. "If the chef decided to cook slowly tonight it won't bother me," she said silkily.

No sooner had the words left her lips than the zing of the elevator let them know that, unfortunately, the chef hadn't been slow and their food was on the way up. Ian glanced across the room and saw the disappointed pout on her lips. Lips he couldn't wait to devour again.

"There's no law that says we have to eat it as soon as the food gets here. It will keep for a while," he assured her.

Her response was a slow, sensuous smile, and a deliberate shifting of her body in the chair exposed a lot more than a bare leg. He bit back the growl that threatened to roar from deep within his throat.

"Don't you dare move," he said when the elevator arrived on his floor. He quickly left and went to the elevator.

Brooke smiled as a shiver slithered through her, and she found she couldn't sit still as he'd instructed. When she had walked into the room and had seen the flickering candles and inhaled the scent of vanilla, as well as seeing Ian standing at the window shirtless, displaying his muscular shoulders and wearing pants that showed what a great butt he had, she had fought back the need to cross the room and touch him all over, ease down on her knees in front of him and unzip his pants and ultimately savor him the same way he'd done her earlier.

With a long sigh she stood and tried to remain calm. Walking around the blackjack table she concentrated on the huge glass window in front of her and the wonderful view of the mountains.

Moments later when she saw Ian's reflection in the glass, she knew he had come back into the room and was standing not far behind her. Their gazes met, reflected in the glass, and she was tempted to turn around.

Her gaze remained fixed on the windowpane as he walked up behind her and wrapped his arms around her. She leaned back into him, letting her head fall back against the breadth of his chest. She felt the need to share herself with him again, not just her body but her heart, whether he wanted it or not. She loved him and nothing could or would ever change that.

"Brooke."

He said her name in that sexy voice of his while nuzzling a certain spot on her neck that could always turn her on. And then she felt his tongue lick the side of her face, moving to the area just below her ear.

"Feel me," he whispered, and she did when she leaned back against him. She felt the hardness of him pressing deep into her backside at the same time she felt him use his hands to part the front of the shirt she wore. And when one of his hands went to her center to claim the area between her legs, a tantalizing sensation shot all through her.

"Are you sure you aren't ready to eat?" he asked huskily.

"I'm sure," she whispered, barely able to get the words out in a coherent voice. His beard was rubbing sensuously against the side of her neck causing an erotic friction that was sending shivers all through her body.

"Then tell me what you're ready for, Brooke."

He turned her around, evidently needing to look into her eyes when she answered. "You, Ian. I'm ready for you."

Her words made something within him shatter and he lifted her to sit on the edge of the blackjack table and then stepped back to remove his pants. He kicked them aside before going back to her and tugging his shirt from her shoulders and tossing it to join his pants on the floor.

He reached out and lifted her bottom and wrapped her legs around him. "I'm ready for you, too, Brooke. Let me show you just how much."

And before she could take another breath he swiftly entered her, going deep and locking tight. And then he began moving with a furor that bordered on obsession. At this very moment they were beating the odds. If anyone had told him that she would be here in his private sanctuary, he would not have believed them. There was no scientific justification for it. But he didn't want to dwell on logical reasoning now. He just wanted to think about making love to her while she teetered on the edge of his private blackjack table.

Tonight he needed this. He needed her.

The only thing he wanted to concentrate on was the

sensations that coursed through him with each and every stroke into her body. His hands at her waist tightened even more and he lifted her almost clear off the green felt tabletop, straining to achieve a more penetrated connection. He leaned forward and kissed her, long and deep, liking the sound of her moan in his mouth. He'd never made love to a woman on a blackjack table before and now in his mind, played the role of a master dealer. But it wasn't his hand he was playing. It was his body over and over into hers, and the last thought on his mind was getting busted. He was on a lucky streak and was determined to come out the winner.

When he broke off the kiss, Brooke looked up at him with eyes glazed with heated desire. And as if their minds had been running along the same thoughts she whispered, "I got a three and a five." She tightened her hold on his shoulders. "Hit me."

A smile touched Ian's lips. He would hit her all right. He tilted her hips on the table at an angle that gave him greater access and thrust deep inside her, aiming for a spot he knew would drive her wild.

It did.

She screamed his name as an explosion hit. The vibration ricocheted through her directly to him. He threw his head back, loving the feel of her orgasm and knowing it would detonate his body as well. When the climax struck, he shuddered uncontrollably and nothing mattered but the woman he was making love to.

She grabbed hold of his face and brought it back down to her, taking his mouth with a hunger that he still felt. His body was getting hard again. When would they get enough? It was as if they were making up for lost time, but he was okay with that. Tonight they needed each other. Tonight they were both winners.

And they would deal with tomorrow when it came.

Seven

"So what do you think?"

Brooke lifted her head from her meal as a blush tinted her cheeks. If Ian was asking her about the food, her reply could be that it was great. If he was referring to their lovemaking sessions, words couldn't describe how wonderful they had been. No matter what happened after she left the Rolling Cascade to return to D.C., she would always cherish every moment she'd spent with him.

She leaned back in her chair. "You know how much I love Thai food, and your chef did a fantastic job. And if you're asking about something else," she said slowly, provocatively, as she picked up her wineglass to take a sip, looking at him over the rim. "All I can say is that I feel I got treated to dessert before the main course." She then gave him a sultry smile.

Ian chuckled low in his throat. "I'm glad everything was to your satisfaction."

He took a sip of wine and thought about how incredibly sexy she looked sitting across from him wearing only his shirt. At least she had buttoned it up.

The primeval male within him wanted to reach out and pull the shirt open. He wanted to once again see how the flickering light from the candles cast a glow against her dark skin.

"It rated higher than my satisfaction, Ian," she said, reclaiming his attention. "You outdid yourself. I don't think I'll ever be able to look at a blackjack table again without blushing."

He shivered at the memory. Hell, when he saw a blackjack table again he wouldn't blush. He would get aroused. Speaking of aroused, he watched how her fingertips skimmed a trail along her wineglass, remembering how her hands had done that to him. Knowing they were headed for trouble if he didn't get his mind off bedding her again, he asked, "What are your plans for tomorrow?"

She grinned. "I won't be going shopping, that's for sure."

"Would you spend the day with me?"

His question surprised her. She would have thought that after tonight he would avoid her at all cost, if nothing else but to see if she was out of his system. She gazed at him thoughtfully as she leaned forward and rested her chin on her hands. "Um, it depends. What do you have planned?"

He smiled. "After an important meeting with my event planner to make sure all the bases are covered for Delaney's birthday party, I'll be free to do whatever I want. Do you have any suggestions?"

They fell silent as Brooke contemplated his question. "Blackjack is definitely out."

He chuckled. "If you say so."

"Um, what about a game of golf?"

He lifted a brow. "Can you play?"

"No, but I'd like to learn. Would you teach me the basics?"

"Yeah, I can do that."

"And I'd like to go swimming in your pool again if you don't mind."

He studied her for a long moment, remembering her in his pool. "I don't mind, but this time I'll take a dip with you."

She stared at him, thinking that was exactly what she had hoped he'd do. "All right." She glanced at her watch then back across the table at him before standing. "It's late. I'd better get ready to go."

He stood, his gaze intense. "Stay with me tonight, Brooke."

Her heart jumped at the invitation, spoken in a deep, husky voice. Her mind was suddenly bombarded with all the reasons she shouldn't, the main one being that if he ever discovered the truth as to why she was staying at the Rolling Cascade, he would consider her actions deceitful.

"I don't think that's a good idea, Ian. We were supposed to be doing the closure thing, remember?" she said softly.

"I remember," he said, coming around the table to stand in front of her. "But at the moment, the only thing I can think about is doing the opening thing with you."

She lifted a brow. "The opening thing?"

A smiled touched the corners of his lips. "Yes, like this," he said, reaching out and working the buttons free on his shirt she was wearing. When the shirt parted he slid his hands over her waist then upward to her chest, tracing his fingertips over the hardened tips of her breasts.

He met her gaze. "Need I say more?"

The gaze that returned his stare shimmered with passion and desire, and when his hand moved lower and touched her between the legs, her breath caught. "No, you don't have to say anything at all," she said after making a soft whimpering sound.

And then she reached out and wrapped her arms around his neck and pulled his mouth downs to hers, deciding they would work on that closure thing another time.

Ian blinked. "Excuse me, Margaret. What did you say?"

Margaret Fields smiled. It was obvious something else had her boss's attention. He definitely was not his usual alert self this morning. He seemed preoccupied. She couldn't help wondering if the others present for their meeting had detected it. "I said that I spoke with Mrs. Tara Westmoreland yesterday and she faxed me her preference for the menu. I've given it to the restaurant that will be handling the catering services."

Ian nodded. "How many people are we expecting?"

"There are three hundred confirmed reservations."

Ian knew that in addition to family and close friends, because of Jamal's status in international circles, a number of celebrities and dignitaries were included in the mix.

"There's a possibility the secretary of state might make an appearance. We'll know in a few days if her schedule will allow it," Margaret said as if in awe of such an event taking place.

Ian then glanced over at Vance. "I take it security is ready to handle things."

Vance smiled. "Yes, and if the secretary does come, I will work with the Secret Service to make sure her stay here is a pleasant one."

Ian knew that Sheikh Prince Jamal Ari Yasir had also reserved a large portion of the resort to house the guests invited to his wife's surprise birthday bash. Ian glanced at his watch. "Okay, keep me informed of anything that develops. Otherwise, it seems everything is under control."

Ian stood. He was to meet Brooke in half an hour and he clearly had no intention of keeping her waiting. "That will be all, and thanks for all of your hard work. I want for us to do everything in our power to make this a special night for the princess of Tahran."

Brooke sighed as she glanced around. The golf course was a lush green, and the open architecture of the massive clubhouse was breathtaking. The redesigned course had been nominated in Golf Digest as one of the best new resort courses, and she could see why. Measuring over eight thousand yards from the back tees, the fairways that wound through large moss-covered hardwoods, oak and pine trees weren't narrow and didn't appear to be squeezed in by the villas.

Ian had told her last night that the first and last holes played along Lake Tahoe and one of the tee boxes was set on a bluff overlooking the water. Nothing detracted from the ambience of the course. Except for the man she was waiting for.

Ian.

Goose bumps suddenly appeared on her body when she thought of how wonderful it was waking up in his arms that morning. Being the Perfect Beginning that he was, they had made love again and she had fallen asleep, only to awaken an hour or so later to find him dressed and leaning against the bedroom door frame watching her.

They had stared across the room at each other for what seemed like an eternity before he finally moved forward, slowly removing his jacket and tossing it aside. Then he reached for her and pulled her up into his arms and kissed her as if his life depended on it. After a long, deep kiss, he'd left, promising to meet her on the walkway in front of the clubhouse at eleven.

Because Ian had also mentioned that the Rolling Cascade's golf club adhered to a dress code, she had visited one of the golf shops earlier to purchase what would be considered the proper attire. From what the salesmen had told her, golf clothes were often bright and colorful, so she had purchased a black top and a lime-green pair of shorts with belt loops, which the salesman claimed was a must. Shorts with cuffs weren't practical because they had a tendency to trap dirt. The salesman had suggested that she purchase a hat with a visor to keep the sun off her face. And arriving at the clubhouse early, she had gone inside to rent a pair of golf shoes.

Brooke turned and recognized the woman walking down the walkway in her direction. She was the person Brooke had bumped into while out shopping yesterday, knocking the shopping bags out of the woman's hands. Brooke, in one of her rare clumsy moments, hadn't been looking where she was going. She'd been captivated by that black lace dress on a mannequin; the one she'd purchased and worn last night.

"Well, hello again," Brooke greeted, smiling when the woman moved to pass her.

The woman eyed Brooke with surprise and to Brooke's way of thinking acted as if they'd never seen each other before. She decided to jog the woman's memory. "Remember me from yesterday?" Brooke said. "I accidentally bumped into you at one of the shops and knocked your packages out of your hand and—"

"Oh, yeah, that's right. I remember now. Sorry about that. My mind was elsewhere," the attractive thirty-something blonde with a British accent said, grasping for a friendlier tone. "Hello to you, too. Sorry, I didn't recognize you," she quickly added, and plastered what Brooke perceived as a fake smile on her face.

Brooke shrugged. "No problem." She then noticed her outfit and the golf shoes she was wearing and asked, "You're about to play a game of golf?"

"Yes, I'm supposed to be meeting my husband in the lobby, and as usual I'm late."

Brooke nodded. "Well, don't let me keep you. Enjoy your game."

"Thanks." And the woman rushed inside the building.

Brooke frowned as she watched the woman walk away. It was as if the woman had no recollection of their earlier collision.

"Hey, beautiful. What's the frown for? You been waiting long?"

Brooke turned and smiled when she saw that Ian had

driven up beside her in a golf cart. "No, I haven't," she said, sliding into the cart to sit beside him.

"Then why the frown?"

"No reason, I guess, other than a lady who I accidentally bumped into yesterday while shopping didn't remember me today. I'm surprised because I practically knocked all the packages out of her hands and had to help her pick them up. She was pretty chatty then."

"What! You mean there's someone who doesn't remember you? That's not possible," he teased. "You're so unforgettable," he said, and grinned as he pulled the cap over her eyes, just seconds before maneuvering the cart around several trees in their paths.

Brooke shifted toward him. "Hey, let's not be a smart-ass," she said chuckling. She couldn't help wondering if he really thought that. Had he had as hard a time forgetting her as she had forgetting him over the years? But then, she'd never tried to forget him. He had remained an integral part of her nightly dreams.

When Ian continued driving for a while, Brooke asked, "Where are you taking me?"

He smiled over at her as he drove around yet another tree. "To my private golfing spot. If I'm going to teach you the game, I don't want any distractions. Golf is like blackjack. You have to be focused."

"Oh." Just hearing him say the word *blackjack* was eliciting memories of the night before. And with those memories came heated lust. She wondered if it would always be that way with them and quickly remembered there wouldn't be any reason for things to be that way because in a week they would part ways and there was no telling when they would see each other again.

Not wanting to think about that, she turned her attention to her surroundings and the cart path they were taking, keeping clear of the greens and teeing grounds.

Finally Ian eased the cart to a stop and she followed his gaze as he took in the area that sat on a bluff overlooking the lake. Brooke glanced at him. "And what am I supposed to do if I hit a ball over into the water?"

He chuckled. "If you're worried that I'd send you to get it, don't be. This is going to be a practice session, and if we lose a ball we play a new one. I brought plenty of them along."

When he climbed out of the cart, Brooke did likewise and waited by his side while he got the golf bag out of the back. She couldn't help noticing how good he looked in his golf shirt and shorts.

He turned to her after placing the straps of the golf bags on his shoulders and said, "Let's go. Oh, by the way, did I mention that golf involves a lot of walking?"

Over the next half hour he explained about golf etiquette, as well as how to score on a scorecard. "Ready to learn how to swing?" he asked, and handed her a club. He then came to stand behind her.

She was about to tell him no, that she wasn't ready and that the nearness of his body pressed against her back would make it impossible to concentrate. But evidently she was the only one with the problem. The close body contact didn't seem to bother him one bit.

Wrapping his arms around her and placing his hands on top of hers, he showed her the proper way to hold the club and swing it. "Just remember," he whispered right close to her ear, "when you're doing a backswing, make sure your body doesn't move more slowly than the club.

And for a downswing," he said, demonstrating, "you don't want your body to move more quickly than your swing. Your club shouldn't play catch-up with your body."

For the next hour they went through a series of swings, some she decided would work for her and some she knew wouldn't. But her golf swings weren't the only thing she was thinking about with Ian almost glued to her back.

"Okay, when do I get to play with the balls?" she asked him, glancing up at him over her shoulder.

"Only you would ask me something with a double meaning such as that at a time like this," he whispered huskily in her ear before pulling her body back to his, letting her know of his aroused state.

She laughed quietly, knowing what balls he was alluding to and moved away from him. "Sorry." She glanced around, trying not to look at him below the belt. "So what's next?"

"Kissing you isn't such a bad idea," he said.

They stood so close that his bare legs brushed lightly against hers. The contact was enough to send heat sizzling through her body, and the fact that he was aroused wasn't helping matters. And when his scent, which had been playing games with her senses for the past couple of hours, finally took hold she parted her lips on a breathless sigh.

That was just the opening Ian needed and he leaned over, and when his mouth touched hers he literally lost it. Never had he needed a kiss more or his common sense less. Now was not a time he wanted to think rationally, since thinking irrationally suited him just fine.

When he'd been teaching her the various golf swings, the feel of her butt against his groin had nearly driven him crazy, overtaken his mind with lust, and he'd been hard-pressed not to do something about it. Even now, if he'd thought for one minute that they had complete privacy, he would be peeling the clothes off her body this very second. He couldn't take the chance, but he could and would make sure they had some private time together later.

His hands tightened around her waist as he continued to kiss her deeply. He knew he had to slow things down a bit, but still, the taste of her was driving him to get all he could because the getting was definitely good.

The sound of a golf cart coming along the path grabbed both their attention, and Ian broke the kiss and took a step back. He glanced over at her and watched as she nervously nibbled her lower lip. Feeling a tightening in his gut, he groaned softly.

Lacking the ability to resist doing so, he cupped her face in his hands and kissed her again. Moments later, pulling back, he rubbed the tip of his finger across her top lip. "You still up for swimming?" he asked, knowing he needed to find the nearest pool to cool off.

"Yes, what about you?"

He chuckled deeply from within his throat. "Yes, I am definitely up for it."

"Ian," she admonished, watching him take a step back to grab the golf bag and place it on his shoulder. But before she could take him to task, he took her hand in his and pulled her toward the cart.

"What about the rest of my lessons?" she asked.

He smiled as her looked at her. "They're coming." Just like you'll be doing pretty soon, he thought as they continued to walk together.

"Can I ask you something, Ian?"

He glanced over at her as they continued walking. "Sure."

"Am I out of your system yet?"

He stopped walking and stared at her. "No. Now you're so deeply embedded there, it's like you've become an ache."

She smiled as they began walking again. She could imagine how much an admission like that had cost him. "Need an aspirin?" she asked coyly.

He stopped walking again and reached up and lightly brushed the side of her face with the palm of his hand. "Now who's being a smart-ass? No, I don't need an aspirin. I just need you, Brooke. And you know what's so scary about that?"

She held his gaze. "No."

"I swore that if I ever saw you again I would avoid you like the plague. But now I can't seem to bear having you out of my sight."

She smiled slowly. "Sounds like we have a problem."

Ian chuckled, although deep down he really didn't find the situation very amusing. "Yeah, it seems that way. Come on. Let's grab some lunch."

"So what sport do you want to try next while you're here?" Ian asked after taking a sip of his soda. He and Brooke were sitting outside on the verandah at one of the cafés enjoying hot dogs, French fries and their favorite soft drinks.

She lifted her gaze from dipping a fry into a pool of ketchup and looked at him, smiling. "It doesn't matter as long as it's not a contact sport."

He laughed. "Are you saying that my touch bothers you?"

"No, it doesn't bother me exactly."

"Then what does it do to you?"

She leaned closer so others sitting around them wouldn't hear. "Makes me hormonally challenged."

A smiled touched the corners of Ian's lips. "Define."

She rolled her eyes. He *would* ask that. She was sure that having such an analytical mind he could definitely figure it out. But if he wanted her to break it down for him, then she would. "Whenever you touch me, or brush up against me, the only thoughts that occupy my mind are those of a sexual nature."

"In other words you get horny?" he asked, seemingly intrigued by her explanation.

"No, Ian. Men get horny. Women become hormonally challenged."

"Oh, I see."

Brooke figured that he did. She couldn't believe the two of them were sitting here having such a conversation while sharing a meal when just a few days ago there had been more bitterness between them than she cared to think about. And yet just as Ian had admitted on the golf course, they were no closer to concluding what they'd once shared than before.

"So what have you been doing for the past four years?" he asked casually, taking another sip of his drink.

Brooke raised a brow. She wasn't stupid. He was really getting around to asking what she hadn't been doing. A woman's body didn't lie, and Ian knew hers better than any man. He was sure after making love to her the night before he had a good idea what she hadn't been doing. "Mainly working. I've had a couple of tough assignments."

Ian nodded. He'd never liked the fact that she was putting her life on the line with every assignment. But he'd had to accept what she did for a living. After all, she had been a deputy when he'd met her. Besides, he had seen her in action a couple of times. She knew how to kick butt when she had to.

"Do you know how much longer you're going to be an agent?" he asked. When they'd talked about marriage, she'd said she would remain an agent until they decided to start a family.

She shrugged. "I'm not sure. Lately I've been thinking that I'm getting too old for field work. I've made my five-year mark, and the undercover operations are beginning to take their toll. I want to get out before I suffer a case of burnout like Dare did."

Ian was about to open his mouth to say something when his cell phone rang. "Excuse me," he said, standing and pulling it from the snap on his belt. "Yes?"

Moments later, after ending the call, he was looking at her apologetically. "Sorry, that was my casino manager. There's a matter that needs my immediate attention."

"I understand."

"We're still on for a swim later? At my place?"

She smiled. "Yes."

"I'll even feed you again."

She chuckled. "It's hard to resist an invitation like that."

"I was hoping that it would be. Let's say around five. Is that okay?"

She nodded. "That's perfect."

"Good." He then leaned over and whispered in her

ear. "And bring an overnight bag so I can help you with that hormonal thing," he said and quickly walked away.

Brooke continued to watch him until he was no longer in sight. It was only then that she released a deep breath. She doubted he would be able to help her with her wacky hormones. If anything, he would probably make them worse. Ian was and had always been too damn sexually potent for his own good. She smiled at the thought of that, since she of all people should know.

She picked up her drink to take another sip when across the verandah a couple sitting at a table caught her eye. It was the woman she had bumped into yesterday. She frowned. There was something about her, but what it was she couldn't quite put her finger on.

Ian had joked about Brooke being an unforgettable person, which she knew wasn't true. But still, she couldn't understand why the woman had not recognized her. Moments later it dawned on Brooke that today her hair was pinned back and she was wearing a hat. Yesterday her hair had been down. That had to be it, she thought. But still, there was something tugging at her brain, something she should be remembering.

Brooke took another sip of her soda, deciding it must not have been important.

Brooke arrived at Ian's penthouse ten minutes early, wearing a very daring, flesh-tone crocheted dress with a see-through bodice. The scalloped hemline was short and showed off the beauty of her legs. Ian knew he was in trouble the moment the elevator door opened.

He took a step back and eyed her up and down. He then pulled in a deep breath. "Hmm. I'm surprised you made it up here in one piece," he said, imagining how many men's eyes had popped out of their heads when they'd seen her. He figured his housekeeping staff was in the lobby mopping up drool as he spoke.

She chuckled as she stepped closer to him and placed her overnight bag down at her feet. "Have you forgotten that I can handle myself?"

No, he hadn't forgotten and had always admired her ability to do so. When she came to stand directly in front of him, the scent of her perfume began playing a number on his libido. He cleared his throat while scanning her outfit again "I thought we were going swimming."

"We are. This time instead of wearing my bathing suit I decided to bring it with me. But I see you're ready."

In more ways than one, he thought, although he knew she was referring to the fact that the only thing he was wearing was a pair of swimming trunks. "Yes, I thought we'd get our swim out of the way and then enjoy dinner. It will be delivered in a couple of hours. But if you'd rather we eat first, then…"

"No, that's fine. I'll probably be quite hungry by then."

He smiled. He intended to make sure she was totally famished. "I'll take that," he said, leaning down to pick up her overnight bag. He looked surprised because the bag was heavy.

She shrugged and smiled. "When have you known me to travel light?"

"Never."

"Then nothing's changed."

He furrowed his brow. "And what about when you're on assignment and you have to travel light?"

"Then I make an exception."

Ian smiled and nodded quietly. "I'll take this up to the bedroom. You're welcome to change in there if you like or you can use one of the guest rooms," he said.

"I'll change in your bedroom."

He moved aside to let her lead the way, and when they got to the stairs and she began climbing ahead of him, his body became more aroused with every step she took. Every time she lifted her foot to move up a step, her short hemline would inch a little higher and emphasize the sweet curve of her bottom.

He pulled back, deciding to just stand there and watch her, or else he would find himself tumbling backward. When she got to the landing she noticed he wasn't behind her and turned around. She lifted a brow when she saw he was still standing on the fourth stair. "Is something wrong?"

"Nothing other than the fact that we need to do something about that dress."

She leaned against the top banister, and he wondered if she knew that from where she was standing with that particular pose, and with the aim of his vision, he could see under her dress. He might be wrong since her outfit was flesh tone and everything seemed to blend in, but he couldn't help wondering if she was even wearing panties.

"What do you suggest we do with it?"

He blinked and met her gaze. His mind had totally gone blank. "Do with what?"

She chuckled. "My dress. You said we had to do something about it."

"We can burn it."

She grinned. "No we can't. It's an exclusive design."

Ian lifted a brow. "Is it?"

"Yes. Don't you like my outfit?"

"A little too much. I suggest you change into your swimming suit before I decide a swim isn't what we both need."

He then began walking up the stairs toward her. When he reached the landing he handed her the overnight bag. "I think this should be as far as I go considering…"

"Considering what?"

"Considering I wouldn't mind taking you right now on that banister you're leaning against." He'd been fantasizing about her every since he'd left her in the café. He'd barely kept his concentration while waiting for her to show up at the penthouse.

She smiled at him as she straightened and gripped the overnight bag. "This should be one interesting afternoon."

He smiled back at her. "Trust me. It will be."

Ian couldn't wait. He had to dive into the pool to cool off. It was either that or change his mind and go upstairs to Brooke. But he knew once he was in that bedroom with her, chances were that's where they would stay until dinner arrived.

He just couldn't get rid of the memory of the two of them on the golf course. Brooke had always been a quick study, and today had been no different. If she practiced there was no doubt in his mind that she would become one hell of a player.

Then there was that point at lunch when he had been tempted to reach out, snatch her up out of her seat and kiss her. Just watching her drink, the way her mouth had fit perfectly around the plastic straw and the way she'd slowly sucked her soda from the cup had made him hard.

He was taking his fourth lap around the pool when he heard her voice. "So you couldn't wait for me."

He glanced over his shoulder and immediately was grateful he was in the shallow end, otherwise he would have clearly sunk to the bottom. Brooke was standing there beside the pool in the skimpiest bathing suit he had ever seen. The one she'd been wearing the other night had been an eye scorcher but this one, this barely there, see-how-far-your-mind-can-stretch piece was definitely an attention getter and erection maker, not that he needed the latter since he was already there.

He pulled himself up and stood in the water and reached out his hand, and in a thick, throaty voice said, "Come here."

Brooke swallowed. When he'd stood, she couldn't ignore how his dripping-wet swimming trunks gave a pretty substantial visual of just how aroused he was. But that didn't keep her from crossing the room, stepping into the pool and taking his outstretched hand.

"You like playing with fire, don't you, Brooke?" he asked when she was standing directly in front of him, so close that their thighs were touching. So close that she could feel his hardness settle against her midsection.

"Not particularly," was the only response she could come up with, since she was so captivated by the dark heat in his eyes.

"Oh, I think you do. And since you like playing with fire I want to see just how hot you can get."

"You already know how hot I can get, Ian," she said, then sucked in a breath when he reached out and wrapped his arms around her waist, bringing her closer to the fit of him.

Ian smiled. Yes he did know. That was one of the things he always loved about Brooke: her ability to let go when they made love and not hold anything back. And speaking of hot…she was like the blast of an inferno, the scorching of volcanic lava, the hottest temperature at the equator. Hell, a summer solstice had nothing on her. And during the four years they'd been apart she hadn't changed.

She'd said she was hormonally challenged, but that was only because her sex life had stopped after him. It didn't take a rocket scientist to figure that one out. When he'd entered her body and found her so tight, he'd known inactivity was the cause. Whatever the reason she hadn't slept with any other man, he intended to remedy that by helping her make up for lost time.

All the reasons why he should be working her out of his system escaped him, probably because at the moment he couldn't think. All the blood from his brain had suddenly rushed downward to settle in the lower part of his body. The part that desperately wanted her.

"I thought we were going to swim," she whispered as he began lowering his mouth to hers.

"We are. Later." And then his mouth devoured hers with all the want and need he'd been holding inside since he'd last made love to her. Had it been just this morning? The hunger that was driving him made it seem a lot longer than that. She had tempted and teased him since then, bringing out the alpha male inside of him.

As usual, she tasted fiery, seductive and spicy. He hungrily consumed her mouth with wanton lust, but kissing her wasn't enough. He reached out and, without breaking the kiss, with a flick of his wrist he undid the tie of her bikini top at her back. Umm, now all that was left was her bottom.

Moments later he pulled back and, kneeling down, grateful they were still in the shallow end, he began peeling the thong bikini down her hips. His hand ran up the length of her inner thigh and he stroked her slowly, liking the sound of her erratic breathing. He stood back up and lifted her hips.

"Wrap your legs around me, Brooke." And the moment she did he slipped between her thighs to widen them and then he buried himself inside of her to the hilt at the same exact moment he buried his tongue inside her mouth.

She sucked in a breath, and with their bodies connected he moved against the pool wall. Of all the places they had made love, they had never made love in a pool. He'd heard that water was a highly sensual playground and he was about to find out if that was myth or a fact. When her back was braced against the wall, he began moving inside of her, flexing his hips, thrusting in and out.

Brooke closed her eyes, absorbing the intensity of Ian moving between her legs. Her fingers bore down on his shoulders as a scream gathered in her throat. He was amazing and was giving her just what she needed. What she wanted. And just seconds before an orgasm was about to hit, he pulled out of her and spun her around with her back to him.

"Lean over and rest your hands on the ledge, sweetheart," he said, whispering in her ear.

The moment she did so he tilted her hips and parted her slightly and pressed into her, entering her from behind. His body went still and he leaned over and kissed her shoulder and asked in a hoarse tone of voice, "You okay?"

"Yes, but do you know what I want?" she asked, gripping the ledge of the pool, liking the feel of his firm thighs right smack up against her butt.

"No, what do you want?"

"More of you. Now!"

She heard him suck in a deep breath just seconds before he began moving. Each stroke was like an electrical charge that sizzled inside her body. She moaned each and every time his hips rocked against her; each contact was a sexual jolt on her mind and her senses.

A guttural sound tore from her throat the same exact moment he screamed her name and gripped her hips tight, holding her steady for his release. And when it came it shot into her womb like a stream of hot molten lava, stimulating each and every part of her body and bringing her to yet another orgasm.

She moaned in surrender, groaned in pleasure and purred with the satisfaction of a kitten just fed. And she knew that no matter what happened once they parted ways, what they were sharing now, this moment, was hers and hers alone. This memory was one that no one could ever take away from her.

Eight

Instead of cooling down, things were only getting hotter and hotter between her and Ian, Brooke thought, almost a week later as she took an afternoon stroll along the lake's edge. Every morning they woke up in each other's arms and she was spending more time at his penthouse than at her villa.

They did almost everything together. He had taken her sailing again, had played a couple of rounds of golf, had taught her how to play poker, and one night they had even gotten together and whipped up dinner in his kitchen.

And they took long walks and talked about a number of things: how they felt about the state of the economy, war and the storms that seemed to get worse each hurricane season. But what they didn't talk about was what would happen after she checked out of the casino on

Sunday, which was only three days away. And she was smart enough to know that things would never be like they used to be between them. No matter how good things were going now, there was no second chance for them. She felt that he would never fully trust her the way he had before they broke up.

For the past couple of days Ian was busier than usual with Delaney's upcoming party. He had asked her to go as his date, and they pretty much decided they would answer his family questions as honestly as possible by saying, "No, we aren't back together. We've decided to be friends and nothing more."

Friends and nothing more.

That thought pierced a pain through Brooke's heart but there was nothing she could do about it. Things had happened just as she'd predicted. In trying to work her out of his system, Ian had only embedded himself deeper in hers. Although she loved him, he didn't love her.

The shrill ring of her cell phone broke into her thoughts and she quickly pulled it out of the back pocket of her shorts. "Hello."

"So, how are things going, Brooke?"

Brooke drew in a deep breath, surprised that Malcolm had called. Their agreement was that he would hear from her only if she had something to report. Within a few days her two-week stay at the Rolling Cascade would be over, and so far, as she'd known he would, Ian was running a clean operation.

"Things are going fine, Malcolm. Why are you calling?"

"I happened to overhear something today that might interest you."

"What?"

"Prince Jamal Ari Yasir is planning a birthday party for his wife there and he plans to present her with a case of diamonds that's worth over fifteen million dollars."

Brooke folded her arms across her middle. "I'm aware of that."

"And how did you come by that information? Not too many people are supposed to know about the diamonds."

"Ian mentioned it. I'm sure you're aware that the sheikh's wife is his first cousin."

"And Westmoreland trusted you enough to tell you about the diamonds?"

Brooke thought about what Malcolm has just asked her. Yes, he had trusted her enough. "He probably thought it wasn't such a big deal. It's not like I'm going to go out and mention it to anyone. And what do the diamonds have to do with the Bureau?"

"Probably nothing, but one of our informers notified our major theft division of a possible heist at the Rolling Cascade this weekend. And the target is those diamonds."

Brooke shook her head. "That's going to be hard to pull off since Ian's security team is top-notch. I've seen their operation. Besides, the jewels arrived this morning and are in a vault that's being monitored by video cameras twenty-four hours a day."

"That might be the case, but we're dealing with highly trained professionals, Brooke. The informer's claiming it's the Waterloo Gang."

Brooke sucked in deeply. "Are you sure?" The Waterloo Gang was an international ring who specialized in the theft of artwork and jewelry and had a reputation for making successful hits. The group was highly mobile, moving from city to city and country to country, and had been on the FBI's most-wanted list for years. Their last hit, earlier this year, had been a jewelry store in San Francisco where over ten million dollars in jewels were taken. Six months ago they had hit a museum in France where artwork totaling over thirty million was stolen.

"We're not sure if our informer's information is accurate. But the Bureau doesn't want to take any chances because such a theft might have international implications. Although Prince Yasir is married to an American, he's still considered a very important ally to this country and we don't want anything to place a strain on that relationship."

Brooked nodded. "I can see where having his wife's birthday present—especially one of such value—stolen might be a lot to swallow."

"And you're sure you haven't noticed anything unusual?"

"Not really. I'd say strange but not unusual. There are some obsessed gamblers, adulterers and someone with a split personality," she said, thinking about the woman she had bumped into while shopping last week. She'd briefly run into her a few times, and certain days she would be friendlier than others; a regular Dr. Jekyll and Ms. Hyde. "Just the kind of characters you'd expect to find at a casino," she concluded.

"Well, notify me if you notice anything. The reason the Waterloo Gang's hits are so well orchestrated and planned is that they have their people in place well in advance, mainly to study the lay of the land, so to speak."

"Will Ian be advised of any of this?"

"Not until we determine if our information is accurate."

Brooke frowned. "That's not good enough, Malcolm. By then it might be too late. He should be told so that he can take the necessary precautions. Don't ask me not to tell him."

For a long time there was a pause, and Brooke hoped Malcolm wouldn't pull rank and demand that she not mention anything to Ian. She was determined to warn Ian what was going on regardless of what Malcolm dictated. If she was fired because of it, then that's the risk she would take.

"Something else you should know is that Walter Thurgood has been assigned to the Waterloo Case," Malcolm said when he finally spoke moments later.

"Why?"

"Because if our informer is right and Thurgood can be credited with stopping a major jewel heist, especially one with possible international connections, that feat would be a great-looking feather in his cap. Someone upstairs is trying like hell to make him look good."

"Yeah, like we don't know who that is," Brooke said sarcastically. "Personally I don't give a damn about him getting credit for anything. I just don't want Ian left in the dark about what might be going on."

"Call me if you notice anything, Brooke, and remember that this is hearsay from an informer. Nothing has been verified yet."

"Okay, and I understand."

Ian smiled, hanging up the phone. Talking to his mother always made him chuckle. It wasn't good enough for Sarah Westmoreland that she now had two married sons, she was still determined to marry the rest of them off in grand style sooner or later.

And today she was ecstatic because Durango had called and said there was a possibility that Savannah might be having twins. An ultrasound was being scheduled in a couple of weeks to confirm or deny such a possibility.

Ian shook his head. He hadn't gotten used to Durango being a husband, much less a father, but that just went to show that some things were meant to be.

Like him and Brooke.

He sighed deeply and walked over to the window in his office. It seemed that today Lake Tahoe was more beautiful than ever. Or maybe he thought that way because he was in such a good mood. And all because of Brooke.

Spending time with her had made him realize that what had been missing in his life was the same thing he'd turned his back on four years ago. But now, waking up with her beside him, gazing into the darkness of her eyes, enjoying a warm good-morning smile was what he needed in his life. But only with her. The time they'd spent together over the past week and a half had been wonderful. He couldn't remember the last time he'd smiled or enjoyed himself more. And then the memories of nights they'd shared in each other's arms could still take his breath away.

Over the years he'd tried to shove her into the past and replace her with more desirable women. However, he hadn't found anyone he desired more or who could replace her in his heart. Just the thought that in three days she would be walking out of his life was unacceptable. He wanted what happened in the past to stay in the past, and he wanted to move forward and reclaim her as his and his alone.

His smile widened when he decided that he would tell her how he felt tonight. He loved her. God, he loved her and would go on loving her. He sighed when that admission was wrung from deep inside of him. He hadn't counted on falling in love with her all over again, and if he were completely honest with himself, he would admit that he'd never stopped loving her. And just to think he'd actually assumed he could work her out of his system. More than anything, he wanted to make her a permanent part of his life.

He walked back over to his desk and picked up the phone. He planned on making tonight one that she wouldn't forget.

"Brooke?"

Brooke was on her way up to see Ian in his office when she turned, following the sound of her name being called, and glanced around. Smiling, she crossed the casino's lobby to give Tara Westmoreland a hug.

"Tara, when did you get here?"

"A few hours ago. Since Jamal asked that I coordinate everything for Delaney's party, I thought it was best for me to be in place a couple of days early. Ian's taking Thorn around, showing him some of the new additions, and I thought I'd just wander around in here and play a couple of the slot machines."

Tara gazed at Brooke with a lift of her brow. "But my question is what are *you* doing here? Did you decide to come up early, too?"

Brooke shook her head, chuckling. "No, I've been here for a week and a half now. I'm here on vacation."

"Hmm," Tara said grinning.

"It's not what you think." Brooke then rubbed a frustrated hand down her face before adding. "At least not really."

As if she understood completely, Tara smiled and took her hand. "Come on. Let's go someplace and have some girls' chat time."

"A strawberry, virgin daiquiri, please," Tara told the smiling waitress.

"And the same for me," Brooke tagged on. Not wanting to jump into a conversation about her and Ian just yet, Brooke asked, "And how do you plan on surprising Delaney?"

Tara chuckled. "Jamal is flying her here straight from Tahran. She believes that he's coming here for an investors' meeting with Ian, Thorn, Spencer and Jared, so seeing me and Thorn, Jared and Dana won't give anything away. She also thinks that Jamal is flying her to France to celebrate her birthday once she leaves here."

She paused when the waitress returned with their drinks. "Most of the family and other invitees will begin arriving that day or the day before. It's going to be up to Jamal to keep Delaney occupied while everyone checks in."

Tara smiled. "One good thing is that everyone is being housed in a separate part of the resort than where Jamal and Delaney are staying. That should minimize the risk of her running into anyone."

"And when will Delaney arrive?"

"Tomorrow."

Brooke took a sip of her drink then asked, "You don't think her seeing me here will give anything away, do you?"

Tara's smile widened. "No. She'll assume, like the rest of us, that you and Ian have finally made amends and are back together." Tara then lifted an arched brow. "Well, is that true, Brooke?"

More than anything, Brooke wished she could say yes. But she couldn't. "No. The only thing Ian and I have managed to do while I've been here is to bury any hostility we've felt and become friends. I feel for us that is a good thing. I care a lot for Ian."

Tara chuckled. "Of course you do. You still love him."

Brooke's cheeks tinted in a blush. "Am I that obvious?"

"Only because I'm in love with a Westmoreland man myself. They seem to grow on you, and once you fall in love with one, it's hard as the dickens to fall out of love…no matter what."

Brooke had to agree. From the first Ian had grown on her and once she fell in love with him that was that. Four years of separation hadn't been able to cure her of being bitten by the love bug. "So what am I supposed to do?"

"Wish I could answer that." Tara leaned in closer and reached for Brooke's arms, squeezing reassuringly. "We all know how smart Ian is, but unfortunately he has a tendency to analyze things to death. But I'm sure once he sits down and considers things rationally, he'll reach the conclusion that you are the best thing to ever happen to him."

Brooke just hoped Tara was right. But then, there was

a lot Tara didn't know, like the real reason Brooke was at the Rolling Cascade. Even if Ian was able to put behind him what happened four years ago, how would he feel if he ever found out that she was now here under false pretenses?

"Don't look now but here come our Westmoreland men," Tara said, breaking into Brooke's thoughts. "I swear they are like bloodhounds on our scent. I doubt there's anywhere we could hide where they wouldn't find us."

Brooke glanced up, and her gaze collided with Ian's as he and his cousin Thorn moved toward their table. Her pulse began beating so wildly that her hand began shaking and she had to put her drink down.

Surprisingly, it was Thorn who pulled her out of her chair to give her a huge hug. Thorn, who used to be the surliest of the Westmorelands, had definitely changed. It seemed that marriage definitely agreed with him. She remembered that at Dare's wedding Thorn and Tara hadn't been getting along any better than she and Ian. Then a few months later she'd received a call from Delaney saying Thorn and Tara were getting married. She had been invited to the wedding, but in consideration of Ian's feelings, she had declined the invitation.

"Did Tara tell you our good news?" he asked Brooke once he released her.

Brooke glanced over at Tara and raised a brow. "No, what news is that?"

"We're having a baby," he announced, grinning broadly.

Brooke rushed around the table and gave Tara a huge hug. "Congratulations. I didn't know."

"We just found out a few days ago, so we haven't told anyone yet," Tara said, smiling over at her husband. Brooke could see the love they shared shining in their eyes.

"Well, I think it's wonderful, and this calls for a celebration, don't you agree, Ian?" Brooke asked, glancing over at him.

He smiled. "Yes, but not tonight since we have special dinner plans."

"Oh." Special dinner plans? This was certainly a surprise to her.

"Meet me at six o'clock in the conservatory, all right?" he asked.

She nodded. "Sure."

Ian then checked his watch. "I hate to run but I have a four-o'clock conference call." He turned to leave.

Brooke knew she needed to tell him about her conversation with Malcolm. "Ian, can we talk for a minute?"

He turned back around and smiled. "I'm in a hurry now, sweetheart, but we'll have time to talk later. I promise." And then he was gone.

Brooke looked down at herself as she stepped into Ian's private elevator. She had decided to wear a pair of chocolate-colored tailored slacks and a short-sleeved beige stretch shirt. Although he'd said it was a special dinner, he had not hinted at how she should dress. Assuming that it would only be the two of them, she figured casual attire would be okay.

It seemed that today the elevator moved a lot faster than it had that first ride up to Ian's special place. Before she could take a deep breath it had stopped at the conservatory.

The door automatically swooshed open, and there he

was, waiting for her. Heat suddenly filled her and he took a step back when she took one forward. Over his shoulder she saw a beautiful, candlelit table set for two. "I hope I'm not too early."

"And I'm glad that you are," he said, and then he leaned down and captured her lips, using his mouth, lips and tongue to churn her brain into mush.

At that moment nothing mattered, not even the thought that all he probably intended for tonight was a chance for them to say goodbye before things got too hectic because of Delaney's birthday party. And if that was his intent, she was fine. She had no regrets about the time she had spent with him these few days.

He released her mouth but kept her close to him, in his arms. "I think we did stand beneath a shooting star that night," he said in a low voice, tracing the tip of his thumb over her lips. "There hasn't been anything but nonstop passion between us since then."

She smiled, thinking of all the times they had spent together since that night, and inwardly she had to agree. "There's always been a lot of passion between us, Ian," she reminded him.

He leaned down and brushed a kiss on her lips. "Yes, things were always that way, weren't they. Do you know that you spoiled me for any other woman?"

"Did I?"

"Yes. I tried to forget you but I couldn't, Brooke."

She sighed. This didn't sound like the goodbye speech she had been expecting. This was a confession. She decided to follow his lead. "I didn't even try forgetting you, Ian. It would have been useless. You were my first lover and a girl never forgets her first."

He grinned. "Sweetheart, the way I see it…or perhaps a better word is the way I *felt* it, I am your one and only. Do you deny it?"

"No. I couldn't stand the thought of another man touching me."

Ian pulled her into his arms. Hearing her admit such a thing touched him deeply.

"Ian?"

He pulled back and looked at her. "Yes?"

"I don't understand why we're talking about these things," she said, confused.

He smiled. "Let's eat and then I'll explain everything."

"Okay, but there's something I need to tell you."

He leaned down and brushed another kiss on her lips. "We'll talk after dinner."

Ian led her over to the beautifully set table and seated her. "Would you like some wine?" he asked, his voice so husky it sent shivers all the way down her spine.

"Yes, please." She watched as he poured the wine in her glass and then in his.

"I had the chef prepare something special for us tonight," he said.

"What?"

He chuckled. "You'll see." And then with the zing sounding on the elevator he said, "Our dinner has arrived."

A half hour later Brooke was convinced there was nothing more romantic than dining beneath the stars; especially when the person you were with was Ian Westmoreland. Dinner was delicious. Melt-in-your-mouth yeast rolls, a steak that had been cooked on an open grill, roasted potatoes, broccoli, the freshest salad to ever touch her lips and her favorite dessert—strawberry cheesecake.

Over dinner he surprised her by sharing with her his dream to open another casino in the Bahamas. He also mentioned the conversation he'd had with his mother earlier and her excitement over the prospect of her first grandchildren being twins.

"I just can't imagine Durango married," Brooke said, shaking her head, thinking about Ian's brother who'd been the biggest flirt she'd ever met. But then, Durango was also a really nice guy and she really liked him.

"Neither could I at first, but after meeting Savannah you'll see why. They may have married because of her pregnancy, but now there's no doubt in my mind that Durango really loves her. So it seems another Westmoreland bachelor has bitten the dust."

"Yes, it seems that way," Brooke said, lowering her head to take another sip of her wine to avoid looking into Ian's eyes. Maybe it was her imagination but she had caught him staring at her a number of times during the course of the evening.

When dinner was over he stood and crossed the room to turn on a stereo system. Immediately, music began playing, a slow instrumental performed by Miles Davis. Ian returned to her chair and stretched out his hand. "Will you dance with me, Brooke?"

Brooke sighed, wondering where all this was leading. The thought that he was going through all this just to tell her goodbye was unsettling, and when he wrapped his arms around her, she placed her head on his chest, fighting back the tears. They'd barely made it through the song when she pulled out of his arms, not able to take it anymore, and took a step back, withdrawing from him.

"Brooke? What's wrong?"

"I'm sorry, Ian, but I can't take it anymore. You didn't have to go through all of this. Why don't you just say the words so I can leave."

Ian lifted a brow. He had planned on saying the words, but for some reason he had a feeling that the words he planned on saying weren't what she was expecting to hear. "And what words do you think I'm going to say, Brooke?" he asked, balling his hands into fists by his side to keep from reaching out to her.

"You know, the usual. Goodbye. *Adios. Sayonara. Arrivederci. Au revoir.* Take your pick. They all mean the same thing in whatever language."

He took a step closer to her. "Um, how about *Je t'aime. Te amo. Kimi o ai shiteru. Nakupenda.* And only because I hear Jamal say it often to Delaney in Arabic, how about, *Ana behibek.*"

He took another step closer as his gaze roamed over her. "But I prefer the plain old English version," he said, reaching out and taking her hand and pulling her close to him. "I love you."

The tears Brooke had fought to hold back earlier flowed down her face. Ian had admitted he loved her. Did he really mean it?

As if reading her mind he tipped her chin up to meet his gaze. "And yes, I mean it. I never stopped loving you, Brooke, although God knows I tried. But I couldn't. Spending time with you this week and a half has been wonderful and it made me realize what you mean to me. I've been living and functioning these past four years, but that's about all. But the moment you walked into my office that day and I breathed in your scent, a part of me knew what had been missing from my life, and this morning when I admitted in my heart what you meant to me, I decided I don't plan to let you ever go again."

Brooke's heart felt like it was going to burst in her chest because she knew if he ever discovered the real reason she'd been here he would feel differently. She knew then that she had to tell him everything. "Ian, there's something I need to tell you. There're things you need to know."

"Sounds serious, but the only serious thing I want to hear is for you to tell me that you love me, too."

"Oh, Ian," she said, reaching up and smoothing a fingertip over his bearded chin. "I do love you. I never stopped loving you, either."

He smiled and pulled her into his arms. "Then as far as I'm concerned, that says it all."

And then he leaned down and gave her a kiss that made everything and every thought flee from her mind.

Brooke awoke the next morning in Ian's bed to find it empty. They had made love under the stars in the conservatory and then they had caught the elevator to his penthouse and made love again in his bed.

She threw the covers off her knowing she had to find him immediately and tell him what was going on. The sooner he knew the better. Half an hour later she ran into Vance, literally, in the lobby.

"Whoa." He grinned, reaching out his arms to steady her. "Where's the fire?"

"Where's Ian, Vance?"

"He's somewhere on the grounds with Jared and Dare. The two of them arrived with their wives this morning." Vance studied her. Saw her anxious look. "Is something wrong, Brooke?"

She sighed deeply. "I hope not, but I think we should take every precaution."

"Okay. Do you want to tell me what it is?"

"Yes, but we have to find Ian first."

Vance nodded. "That's not going to be a problem," he said, taking his mobile phone out of his jacket. He punched in one number and said, "Ian? You're needed. Brooke and I are on our way to your office. Meet us there."

Vance then clicked off the phone, placed it back in his jacket, smiled and gently took hold of Brooke's arm. "Come on. He's on his way."

Ian arrived a few minutes after they did. He walked in with Dare. Dare Westmoreland was tall and extremely handsome just like all the Westmoreland men. At any other time Brooke would have been glad to see her mentor, but at the moment she preferred not having an audience when she told Ian everything; including why she's been there for the past week and a half. She quickly concluded that now would not be the best time to tell him that particular part of it. She would tell him that later. But she needed to tell him about her conversation with Malcolm.

She gladly accepted the huge hug Dare gave her. The Westmorelands were big on hugs, and she always accepted any they gave her with pleasure. As soon as Dare released her, Ian moved in and circled his arms around her. He had a worried look on his face. "Brooke, what's wrong? Are you all right?"

She smiled. "Yes, I'm fine, but I found out something

yesterday that you should know. I tried telling you last night but..." She lowered her head, studying the ceramic tile floor, knowing he knew why she'd stopped talking in midsentence and also felt that Dare and Vance had a strong idea, as well.

"Okay, you want to tell me now? Or is it private between the two of us?" he asked in an incredibly low and sexy voice.

She raised her head and met his gaze. "No, in fact Vance needs to hear it and Dare might be able to lend some of his experience and expertise."

Ian frowned. "This sounds serious."

"It might be," she replied.

"Then how about you tell us what's going on."

For the next twenty minutes she repeated her conversation with Malcolm. Most of it, anyway. It would have taken less time if Dare and Vance hadn't interrupted with questions. Both Dare and Vance had heard of the Waterloo Gang.

Ian turned to Vance. "What do you think?"

Vance's face was serious. "I think we should do as Brooke suggested and take additional precautions."

Ian nodded. "I agree." He then turned to Brooke. "According to what you've said, it's this gang's usual mode of operation to set up shop within their targeted site, right?"

"Yes."

"That means they're probably already here then," he said, and she could hear the anger in his voice.

Brooke nodded. "More than likely. But keep in mind nothing has been confirmed yet. The Bureau is still checking out this informer's claim."

"In that case," Dare said, "who gave you the author-ity to share this information with Ian?"

Brooke met Dare's gaze. She knew what he was asking her and why. "No one gave me the authority, Dare. I felt Ian should know. Even if it's not true at least he should be prepared."

"And if it is true," Vance said, his voice thickening with anger, "then we'll be ready for them."

Ian sighed. "And let's make sure of it. Come on. We need to get up to the surveillance room."

When Vance and Dare turned toward the elevator, Ian called over his shoulder, "You two go ahead. Brooke and I will be there in a minute."

Once Vance and Dare had left, Ian crossed the room to sit on the edge of his desk. He drew in a deep breath as he continued to look at her. Then giving her a ques-tioning look, he said, "You're extremely nervous about something. There's more isn't there? There's something you aren't telling me."

Brooke sighed. She knew the time of reckoning had arrived. For a moment she didn't say anything and then, "Yes. I didn't want to say anything in front of Vance and Dare."

He nodded. "Okay, what is it?"

She lifted her chin a notch and met his direct gaze. "There's a reason I've been here at the casino this past week and a half, Ian."

He frowned. "So you weren't here for rest and relax-ation like you claimed?"

She shook her head. "No."

Silence surrounded them for a moment and then Ian asked, "You tracked the Waterloo Gang here?"

Her expression became somber. "No, it had nothing to do with the Waterloo Gang," she said, walking over to the window and looking out, trying to hold on to her composure.

He raised a brow. "Then what?"

She turned back to him. "You. I was asked to come here to make sure you were running a clean operation. But at no time did I—"

"What!" he said, coming to his feet. "Are you standing there saying that you were sent here to spy on me and that all those times we spent together—days and nights—meant nothing to you other than you doing your job? That I was nothing but an assignment?"

Brooke quickly crossed the room to him. "No! That's not what I'm saying. How could you think that? It really wasn't an official assignment and—"

"I don't want to hear anything else!" Ian said in a voice that shook with anger.

"Ian, please let me explain things to you," Brooke said, reaching out to grab hold of his hand.

He flinched. "No. I don't think you need to say anything more. You've pretty much said it all."

Nine

Both Vance and Dare glanced up when Brooke walked into the security surveillance room. Vance lifted a brow. "Where's Ian?"

Brooked shrugged as she approached the two men. "Not sure. He left a couple of minutes before I did."

They nodded, too polite to probe any further. "I'm having my men run the tapes of the vault to see if there's any particular person or persons who made frequent trips over in that area," Vance said.

He then turned to the man sitting at a monitor. "Show us what you have, Bob."

Before Bob could pull anything up, Ian walked in. Although everyone glanced his way, no one said anything. It was obvious from his expression that he wasn't in the best of moods. Vance explained to Ian what they were doing.

"Okay, Bob, let her roll," Vance said.

They viewed over thirty minutes of footage, and nothing stuck out to arouse their suspicions. At one point, Brooke glanced over her shoulder and found Ian staring at her. The look in his eyes nearly broke her heart. Whatever progress they had made over the past week had been destroyed. The man who had expressed his love for her last night looked as if he resented her in his sight today.

"Hold it there for a moment," Vance said to Bob, breaking into Brooke's thoughts and claiming her attention. "Give me a close-up."

The monitor zeroed in on the red-haired woman's facial features. Vance shrugged and said, "Okay, move on. I thought for a second she reminded me of someone."

Brooke, who had been sitting in an empty chair beside Dare, stood, her mind alert. She stared at the woman they had just brought up on the screen. "Hey, wait a minute."

Dare glanced up her. "What?"

"I've got a funny feeling."

Dare chuckled and said, "If history serves me correctly, that means she might be on to something."

Brooke glanced over at Vance. "Can we do a scan of the casino for a minute?"

Vance nodded to Bob, and the man switched to another monitor that showed the occupants who were milling around in the casino. Dare laughed. "I see my wife is spending money as usual," he said, when the scanner picked up a pregnant Shelly Westmoreland strolling into a gift shop.

"Can you give us a clue as to what we're looking for?" Ian asked in an agitated tone.

Brooke glanced over her shoulder. "Remember that woman I mentioned last week that I bumped into while shopping and who didn't remember me the next day?"

"What about her?" Ian asked.

"I've always found it strange that every time I ran into her in the casino she acted different. I always got bad vibes from her. It seemed as if she had a split personality."

"Could be she was just a moody person," Vance interjected.

"Or you may have run into her on her bad days," Dare added.

Brooke nodded. "Yes, but there were other things, and something in particular that I just can't put my finger on," she said, tapping her fingers on the desk. Then she remembered.

"That first day I bumped into her and accidentally knocked packages out of her hand, she mentioned she was on her way somewhere but not to worry because she was known to always be an early bird and that she would be on time for her appointment. The next day I saw her at the golf course, she mentioned being habitually late everywhere she went."

Brooke turned her attention back to the monitor and watched as it continued to scan all the occupants in the casino. "Okay, Bob," she said, moments later. "There she is. The blonde standing next to the tall guy with shoulder-length black hair. That's supposed to be her husband."

By this time, everyone's curiosity was piqued and they stood staring at the monitor.

"Do a profile check, Bob, to see who they are," Vance instructed when the screen had zeroed in on the couple's faces. Moments later information appeared on the screen. The woman was Kasha Felder and the man, Jeremy Felder. They lived in London. Both had clean records, no prior arrests or violations. Not even a parking ticket.

"Now go back and run a profile check on the woman with the red hair."

Bob quickly switched screens. "Um, that's strange. I'm not coming up with an ID on her. It's like she doesn't exist."

Brooke nodded and glanced up at Vance. He now knew where she was going with this. "Scan both women's facial structures," Vance instructed.

Moments later, it was evident that even with different color hair, the women had the same facial structure. A more detailed breakdown showed the woman with red hair was a natural blonde and she was wearing a wig.

Ian came to stand beside Brooke. "Same woman?" he asked, frowning.

Brooke shook her head. "No, I don't think so."

He glanced over at her, lifting a brow. "Twins then?"

"More than likely, which would explain my split-personality theory. But I have a gut feeling there's more." She glanced over at Vance. "Can we look at the tapes around the vault from last week?"

Vance smiled. "Certainly."

Brooke chuckled. She could almost imagine the adrenaline running in the older man's veins. He probably hadn't experienced this much excitement since leaving the nation's capital.

For the next thirty minutes they scanned the footage. Ian, who was still standing beside her, asked, "Just what are we looking for now?"

She glanced up at him and immediately felt her pulse jump at his closeness. "A third woman."

Dare raised a brow. "Triplets?"

"Possibly," she said. "These two are wearing bracelets on their right wrists. One day I happened to notice that she was wearing a bracelet on her left arm." Moments later she told Bob, "Back it up a second and slow it down." Then, "Okay, hold it right there. The lady with the dark-brown curly hair. Let's zero in on her for a second."

Bob did, and after they viewed the facial structure, it showed conclusive evidence they were viewing three different women with identical facial structures. All with natural blond hair. Triplets.

"Damn," Vance said. "No wonder they can pull those hits off. We're dealing with triplets, and no telling who else is tied in to their operation."

Ian turned to Vance. "Do you think they have an inside accomplice?"

"That's how it works most of the time." He then turned to Bob. "Okay, let's go through the footage for the past week and a half. I want to concentrate on all three women. What I want to know is whether or not they meet up with any of our employees, no matter how casual it appears."

Three hours later they had their answers. The triplet with the brown curly wig had met on two occasions with Cassie, who worked in the casino's business office. In one piece of footage, Cassie was even seen handing the woman an envelope.

"I think we've seen enough, don't you?" Ian said with anger in his voice.

"Yes," Vance said, shaking his head. "For now. Let's

get Cassie in here and ask her a few questions. She's only twenty-three and the thought of jail time, especially in a federal prison, should shake her up. I bet she'll end up spilling her guts to save her skin."

"Then what?" Ian asked, shaking his head as he remembered all the times the young woman had tried to come on to him.

Vance smiled. It was apparent to everyone that his mind was already working, going through numerous possibilities. "And then we set a trap for the Waterloo Gang. One that will put them out of operation permanently."

Vance had been right. Fearful of jail time, Cassie had confessed, explaining that she had met a man in the casino by the name of Mark Saints, a Brit who wanted to have a good time. She had gone to his room one night and ended up getting drugged. While she was unconscious, Mark had taped a damaging video which he used to blackmail her into doing what he needed her to do—provide the information he needed about the jewels and the setup of where the vault was located.

Cassie didn't know much about anything else, specifically how the heist would be carried out. However, she did mention Mark and a woman claiming to be his sister were particularly interested in the security system and the location of the video cameras.

It was late afternoon by the time Brooke had left the security surveillance room, no longer able to handle Ian's contempt. She was walking across the lobby when she heard her name being called and turned and smiled when she saw Tara, Shelly and another woman she didn't know. Introductions were made and she discovered the other woman was Dana. Dana was married to Ian's brother, Jared. She had a beautiful and friendly smile and Brooke liked her immediately.

"Would you like to join us for dinner?" Shelly asked, smiling. "It seems we've been dumped by our husbands. They plan to hit the poker tables and then go up to Ian's penthouse to see what other trouble they can get into."

Brooke smiled. "Sure, I'd loved to." For the past several days she'd eaten dinner with Ian, but she had a strong feeling that he wouldn't want her company this evening or any other evening. She then glanced around. "Has Delaney arrived yet?"

Tara chuckled. "Yes, they got in around noon today."

"And you still aren't worried about her running into anyone?"

A grin touched the corners of Tara's lips. "No. Jamal has been given strict orders to keep his wife occupied for the next couple of days, and I have a feeling he's more than capable of doing that. Delaney won't be leaving her room anytime soon…if you know what I mean."

Brooke shook her head, grinning. Yes, she had a pretty good idea just what Tara meant. "Isn't she pregnant?"

Tara nodded and said seriously, "Yes, but trust me, that has nothing to do with it. Even after five years of marriage, the attraction between Delaney and her desert sheikh is so strong, keeping her behind close doors for forty-eight hours will be a piece of cake for Jamal."

Brooke enjoyed having dinner with the three women. Afterward, they left the restaurant to check out the various shops, especially the lingerie boutique in the lobby. Deciding to call it an early night she departed their company and was in her room before nine o'clock.

She took a leisurely soak in the Jacuzzi and then slipped into a nightgown.

A trap had been set and if everything worked out the way they hoped, they would catch the Waterloo Gang red-handed trying to steal the jewels Jamal was to present to Delaney Saturday night.

Brooke had made a decision that once the gang was apprehended, she would leave and not attend Delaney's birthday bash. She was to go as Ian's date, but she figured she would be the last person he would want to show up with.

As she settled in bed, tears she couldn't hold back rolled down her cheeks. If only Ian would have let her explain. But he hadn't. He had refused to listen to anything she had to say in her defense. Once again he saw her as a very deceitful person. He didn't trust her, and without trust, love was nothing.

"Hey, Ian. You want to play blackjack with us?"

Ian refused to turn around from his stance in front of his penthouse window. Instead he closed his eyes as memories of the night he had made love to Brooke on the same blackjack table at which Jared, Dare and Thorn were seated raced through his mind.

"Ian?"

He recognized the concern in Jared's voice. Being the firstborn, Jared had been bestowed with the dubious responsibility of looking out for his younger siblings. And now, thirty-plus years later, nothing had changed.

Deciding it was best to give him an answer, he turned around and said, "No, you all go ahead and play without me." He couldn't help but smile when he saw the look of relief on their faces. He was a natural ace when it came to blackjack and they all knew it.

"One of you act as dealer while I talk to Ian for a while," Dare said to the others.

Ian raised his eyes to the ceiling. Dare, being the oldest of all the Westmoreland men—although he was only older than Jared by a few months—had always felt responsible for his younger siblings and cousins. He'd always taken being "the oldest" seriously, but at times he could be an outright pain in the rear end. Ian pretty much figured this would be one of those times.

"We need to talk," Dare said when he approached him.

"If it's about Brooke *we* have nothing to say," Ian said before taking a sip of his drink.

"The hell we don't. So let's go somewhere private."

Ian figured he wouldn't be able to get Dare off his case until he complied with his request, and figured the sooner he did so, the better off he'd be. "Fine. We can go into my office."

Dare followed Ian to the room he'd set aside as a small office and closed the door behind them. Ian moved to sit down behind his desk while Dare chose to stand in front of it with his hands on his hips and his expression anything but friendly.

"Say what you have to say, Dare, so we can get this over with," Ian said, setting his glass aside.

Dare leaned over to make sure he could be heard. "For a man who's extremely smart you're not acting very bright."

Ian's lips curled into a smile. Leave it to Dare to speak his mind. "Why? Because I refuse to let the same woman break my heart twice?"

"No, because twice she's looked after your best interest and you're too blind to see it. I know what has you pissed with her, but if you would have given her the chance to explain, she would have told you that if she hadn't agreed to come here to make sure things were running smoothly, they would have sent the federal agent from hell. Although she knew how you felt about her, she came anyway because she trusted you and knew she wouldn't find anything wrong with your operation."

Ian sat back in his chair in a nonchalant posture. "Did she tell you that?"

"No, Vance did."

Ian sat up. "Vance? How the hell does he know anything?"

"Because of his connections within the Bureau. He didn't buy her story of just being here on vacation, so he made a few calls. He approached her while you were out of town and of course she didn't let on to anything. And before you ask, the reason Vance didn't tell you of his suspicions is because he didn't see Brooke as a threat, especially after she told him…and I quote, "No matter what you or anyone else might think, I trust Ian implicitly."

When Ian didn't say anything, Dare continued. "I don't know of too many men who can boast of such loyalty from a woman. But you can, Ian." Without saying anything else, Dare turned and walked out of the room.

Ian remained where he was, sitting in silence while he thought about everything Dare had said. He stood and began pacing the room, replaying in his mind all the times he'd spent with Brooke since she'd arrived at the Rolling Cascade, and he knew Dare was right. She had come here to look out for his best interest.

He rubbed a hand down his face. Why did love have to be so damn complicated? And why was he so prone to letting his emotions rule his common sense where Brooke was concerned? Mainly because he loved her so much. Deep down a part of him was afraid to place his complete heart on the line. But he would. He knew what he had to do. He had to swallow his pride and surrender all.

He moved to the door with an urgent need to see Brooke, wondering if she was downstairs in the casino. His cell phone rang and he stopped to answer it. "Yes?"

"This is Vance. It seems they're going to make their move earlier than planned."

Ian understood. "Is everything in place?"

"Down to the letter. It's like watching a movie and I've saved you a front-row seat."

"I'm on my way."

He quickly walked out of his office and glanced over at Dare. "It seems the triplets are about to put their show on the road. Come on."

Ten

Ian's gaze lit on Brooke the moment he and Dare walked into the security surveillance room. He wanted to go to her, ask her forgiveness and tell her how much he loved her, but knew it was not the time or the place.

Even so, he couldn't help studying her. It wasn't quite eleven o'clock, however it appeared as if she'd been roused out of bed. She had that drowsy look in her eyes, although he knew that with what was going down, she would be alert as a whip.

Knowing that if he continued to stare at her, he would eventually cross the room and kiss her, he fought the temptation and turned to Vance. "Okay, what do we have?"

Vance chuckled. "They did just as we figured they would. They placed the video monitors in a frozen mode so the images my men are seeing are images from three hours earlier. Unknown to our intruders we installed additional video cameras and are able to see everything they're doing. Take a look."

Ian came to stand before the monitor. He saw two figures dressed in black as they silently moved across the room toward the vault. "Where's the third woman? And the guy?"

"They're in the casino," Brooke answered, and Ian could tell she was deliberately not looking at him. She pointed to another monitor that brought the couple into view. "What they're doing is establishing an alibi," she explained. "For the past hour they have been hopping from table to table, playing blackjack, poker, talking with the casino workers, anything they can do to make sure they're seen. Their alibi would be it's impossible to be in two places at the same time."

"It's possible if you're dealing with identical triplets," Dare said, frowning. "But then, no one was supposed to know that."

Ian shook his head. The foursome could have pulled this off as the perfect jewel heist if Brooke hadn't suspected something with that woman. No longer able to fight the urge any longer, he moved to stand beside Brooke and heard the sharp intake of her breath when he did so.

"Did we ever find out why we couldn't pick up a solid ID on the other two triplets?" he asked Vance.

"Yes. It seems they were separated at birth and raised by different families. They hooked up while in college, and nothing is recorded of them getting into any trouble. In fact, all three are from good homes. One of their adoptive fathers is a research scientist in Brussels."

He shook his head and continued. "It's my guess

they're doing this for kicks to see if they can get away with it. For four years they have eluded the law, which has made them bolder and bolder and almost unstoppable." A smile lit Vance's eyes when he added, "Until they decided to do business in my territory."

Everyone crowded around the monitor and watched as the two figures tried their hands at getting inside the vault. "They have successfully bypassed the alarm, which makes me think that one of them is a pro at that sort of thing," Brooke said.

Ian knew he didn't have to ask if their security men were in place. What the two intruders didn't know was that once they entered the vault, they would trigger a mechanism that would lock them inside.

He decided to move away from Brooke. Her scent was playing havoc with his mind and had aroused him to a high degree. He walked over to stand beside Dare, who was watching the activity on the monitor intently. Just as Ian knew this was not the time and place to kiss Brooke, he also knew it wasn't the time and place to thank his cousin for taking him to task, making him realize what a jewel he had in Brooke.

"See that wristwatch blondie is wearing," Brooke said, indicating the blond woman who was standing with her husband and chatting with one of the casino workers. "It's my guess it relays signals to and from the two who are working the vault. If something goes wrong she'll be the first to know."

"And my men will be ready if they try anything," Vance said. "All eyes are on them. In fact the woman that blondie is being so chatty with is one of my top people. She's pretending to be a casino worker tonight."

Ian shook his head. "Damn, Vance, you thought of everything."

Vance laughed. "That's why you pay me the big bucks."

They watched as the vault door opened. The kicker to the trap was to make sure both women went inside the vault. To make sure they did, Vance's team had put fake jewels in a big box that would require both of the women to lift it to stuff the jewels into the black felt bags they were carrying.

The plan worked. The moment both women were inside, the door slammed shut behind them. Everyone switched their gazes from that monitor to the one of the casino. And just as Brooke predicted, they read the look of panic on blondie's face when she received a signal from her sisters that something was wrong.

They watched as the woman leaned over and whispered into her husband's ear, not knowing her every word was being picked up. "Something went wrong. I got a distress signal from Jodie and Kay." The couple turned, no doubt to make their great escape, and barged right into several security men who were waiting to arrest them.

Vance grinned and said, "Those two are taken care of, so let's go meet and greet the other two."

Two hours later Ian's office was swarming with the local FBI and the news media. Everyone wanted to know how Ian's security team had been able to pull off what no law officials could—finally end the reign of the Waterloo Gang.

"I have to credit an off-duty FBI agent who just

happened to be vacationing at the Rolling Cascade," Ian said into the microphone that was shoved in his face. "This agent was alert enough to notice something about one of the women that raised her suspicions. She brought it to me and my security manager's attention. Had she not, we would have suffered a huge loss here tonight. I'm sure Prince Yasir is most appreciative."

Ian glanced around, but he didn't see Brooke any-where and figured with all that had gone down, she was probably in one of the lounges getting a much-needed drink. "I also have to thank my cousin, Sheriff Dare Westmoreland, who just happens to be visiting from Atlanta. He helped us figure things out."

Ian then glanced over at Vance and grinned. "And of course I have to credit the Rolling Cascade's security team for making sure we had everything in place to nab the Waterloo Gang and to obtain the evidence we need to make sure they serve time behind bars. The entire thing was captured on film. We have handed the tapes over to the local FBI."

Ian checked his watch. It was almost two in the morning. More than anything he wanted to find Brooke, talk to her, beg her forgiveness, kiss her, make love to her…

"Mr. Westmoreland, were you surprised the Waterloo Gang was triplets?"

"Yes." And that was the last question he was going to answer tonight. He needed to see Brooke. "If you have any more questions, please direct them to Vance Parker, my security manger. There's a matter I need to attend to."

Ian caught the elevator down to the lobby and quickly

looked around. He released a sigh of relief when he saw Tara and Thorn at one of the slot machines. Before he could ask them if they'd seen Brooke, an excited Tara asked, "Is the rumor that we're hearing true? Did your security team actually nab a bunch of jewel thieves?"

"Yes, with Brooke's and Dare's help." Ian glanced around, his gaze anxiously darting around the crowd. "By the way, have either of you seen Brooke lately?"

Tara's smile turned to a frown. "Yes, I saw her a few moments ago. She was leaving."

Ian nodded as he eyed the nearest bank of elevators. "To go up to her room?"

"No, leaving the casino."

He snatched his head back around to Tara and a deep frown creased his forehead. "What do you mean she was leaving the casino?"

Tara narrowed her gaze at him. "Just what I said. She was checking out. She apologized to me for not staying for Delaney's party, but she said that she felt under the circumstances it was best if she left. She then got into her rental car and drove off."

"Damn." Ian rubbed the tension that suddenly appeared at the back of his neck. "Did she say where she was going?"

Tara glared at Ian and placed her hands on her hips. "Maybe. But then why should I tell you anything. You had your chance with her, Ian Westmoreland. Twice."

Ian glared back and then he looked at Thorn for help. His cousin merely laughed and said, "Hey, don't look at me. That's the same look she gives me before telling me to go sleep on the couch."

Ian bit back a retort that, considering Tara's condition, it seemed Thorn hadn't spent too many nights on the couch. He shook his head. He knew how loyal the women in the Westmoreland family were to each other, and there was no doubt in his mind that they had now included Brooke in their little network. That was fine with him because he intended to make a Westmoreland woman out of her—however, he had to find her to do so.

But first he had to convince Tara that he was worthy of Brooke's affections. "Okay, Tara, I blew it. I know that now. I owe Brooke a big apology."

She rolled her eyes and cross her arms over her chest. "That's all you think you owe her?"

He drew in a deep breath in desperation. "And what else do you have in mind?"

"A huge diamond would be nice."

Ian thought about strangling her but knew he would have to deal with Thorn. Although Ian would be the first to admit that Thorn had mellowed some since he'd gotten married, nobody in their right mind would intentionally get on Thorn's bad side.

"A huge diamond is no problem. She deserves a lot more than that."

Tara studied him as if she was considering his words. Then she asked, "And do you love her?"

"Yes." He didn't hesitate in answering. "More than life itself, and I just hope she'll forgive me for being such a fool."

Tara shrugged. "I hope she will, too. She looked pretty sad when she left here tonight and nothing I said could convince her to stay."

Ian nodded and thought he'd try his luck again by asking, "And where did she go?"

Tara looked at him for a long moment before saying, "To Reno. She couldn't get a flight out tonight so she's going to stay at a hotel in Reno and fly out sometime tomorrow."

Panic gripped Ian. He was beginning to come completely unraveled. "Do you happen to know which hotel?"

Tara took her sweet little time in answering. "The Reno Hilton."

With that knowledge in hand, Ian was out of the casino in a flash.

"Yes, Malcolm, I'm fine," Brooke said, biting down on her bottom lip to keep from crying. "No, I'm not at the casino. I'm at a hotel in Reno," she added when he asked her whereabouts. "I'll be flying home tomorrow."

Moments later she said, "It's a long story, Malcolm, and I don't want to go into details tonight. I'll call you when I'm back in town and we'll talk then."

Brooke hung up the phone. According to Malcolm, everyone at national headquarters was blissfully enjoying the news of the capture of the Waterloo Gang. The director wanted to meet with her to express his special thanks. Everyone was celebrating. That is, everyone but Walter Thurgood. From what Malcolm had said, the man was pretty pissed off that he wasn't able to get the credit. In a way, she was glad things had worked out the way they did. Had Thurgood shown up he would have tried to throw his weight around. But she, Dare and Vance had proven to be a rather good team. And then there was Ian.

Ian.

Just thinking his name brought a deep pain to her

heart. During the course of the night, she had felt his eyes on her, and each time when she imagined what he thought of her, her heart would break that much more. As she'd tried explaining to Tara, who'd tried to talk her out of leaving the Rolling Cascade, there was no way she could stay there any longer with Ian thinking the worst of her.

She glanced up when she heard a knock on her hotel room door. She crossed the room wondering who it could be at this hour. It was past three in the morning. "Yes?"

"It's Ian, Brooke."

Her heart began pounding hard in her chest. Ian? What was he doing here? Had he followed her all the way to Reno just to let her know, again, how little he trusted her? Well, she had news for him. Whether he wanted to believe it or not, she hadn't done anything wrong and she refused to put up with his attitude any longer.

After removing the security lock she angrily snatched open the door. "What are you doing—"

Before she could finish getting the words out, a single white rose was placed in her face, followed by a red one. When he lowered the roses she saw him standing there. She had to take a full minute to catch her breath.

"I'm here to ask your forgiveness, Brooke, for a lot of things. May I come in?"

She didn't answer. Instead, after a couple of moments she stepped aside. When he walked passed her, her body began humming the moment she caught his masculine scent. Once he stood in the middle of her room, she closed the door and turned to face him. He looked as tired as she felt, but even with exhaustion lining his features, he looked extremely good to her.

"Is the media still at the casino?" she decided to ask when it appeared he was trying to get his thoughts together.

"Yes, they're still there. I left them in Vance's capable hands."

She nodded. "I would offer you something to drink but…"

"That's fine. There's a lot I have to say, but I don't know where to start. I guess the first thing I should say is that I'm sorry for being so quick to jump to conclusions. I'm sorry for not trusting you, not believing in you. My only excuse, and it's really not one, is that I love you so much, Brooke, and I was scared to place that degree of love into your hands again. I hurt so badly the last time."

"Don't you think I was hurting as well, Ian?" she asked quietly. "It wasn't all about you. It was about us. I loved you enough to do anything to protect you. And over the years, nothing changed. If I hadn't still loved you as much as I did, I would not have cared if the Bureau sent someone to prove what I already know. You're an honest man who wouldn't do anything illegal."

She breathed in deeply before she continued, "This week has been real. My feelings and my emotions were genuine. I wasn't using you to find out information. The very idea that you thought I had…"

Ian crossed the room and cupped her face in his hands. "I admit I was wrong, sweetheart. Call me stupid. Call me a fool. Call me overly cautious. But I'm here asking, begging for you to give me, us, another chance. My life is nothing without you in it. I've seen that for four years. I love you, Brooke. I believe in you. I made a huge mistake, one I plan to make up for during the rest of my life. Please say you forgive me and that you still love me."

She looked deeply into his eyes. Placing the roses on the table she reached up and covered his hands with hers. "I love you, Ian, and I forgive you."

A rush of relief flooded from him just seconds before he lowered his face to hers and captured her lips. He kissed her long, hard, deep, needing the connection, the affection, and the realization that she was giving him, giving them, another chance. Coming here had been his ultimate gamble. But it had paid off.

When she wrapped her arms around his shoulders he picked her up into his arms. He needed to touch her, taste her, make love to her. He needed to forge a new beginning for them that included a life together that would last forever. Knowing there was only one way to get the closeness, that special connection that he craved, he walked over to the bed and placed her on it. Love combined with hunger drove him. He knew he had to show her just how much she meant to him. How much he loved her.

Pulling back slightly, he began trailing kisses along her neck and shoulders as he began removing the clothes from her body. Moments later he dragged in a deep breath when he had her completely undressed. He stood away from the bed and stared at her, absorbing into his physical being every aspect of her that he loved and cherished.

After removing his clothes he returned to the bed and pulled her closer to him. "I love you, Brooke. I didn't realize how much until I spent time with you these past two weeks. And I knew then that we were meant to be together."

"And I love you, too," she whispered when he cupped her butt and pulled her against the throbbing heat of his erection. And then he was kissing her again, putting into action what he'd said earlier in words. Love was driving him, propelling him to taste every inch of her, feel her moaning and writhing and whimpering under his lips. And when he knew she couldn't take any more, he stretched his body over hers, ran his fingertips down her cheek and whispered, "I love you," just seconds before he drove into her, connecting their bodies as one. And then he began moving, rocking, pushing her toward a climax so powerful he had to fight back the spasms that wanted to overtake him in the process.

Meticulously, methodically and with as much precision and love as any one man could have for any woman, Ian made love to her, igniting urges and cravings to explosive degrees. He took his time, wanting her to feel the love he was expressing. He wanted to show her that she was the only woman he wanted, the only one he could and would ever love.

"Ian!"

And when the explosion hit, skyrocketed them into another world, he held on and groaned when his release shot deep into her body. And when she bucked and tightened her legs around him he knew he was where he would always belong.

When they came back down to earth he pulled her into his arms, needing to hold her. He closed his eyes briefly, knowing this was paradise and heaven all rolled into one. Then he opened his eyes, knowing there was one other thing he had to do to make his life complete.

Rising up over her, he looked into the eyes of the woman he loved. "Will you marry me, Brooke? Will you share your life with me forever?"

He saw the tears that formed in her eyes, saw the trembling of her lips and heard the emotion in her voice when she whispered, "Yes. I'll marry you."

Smiling, he leaned down and rubbed his bearded face against her neck, knowing he was the happiest man in the world. He pulled back and, still smiling deeply, he said, "Come here, sweetheart."

And then he was pulling her into his arms again, intent on making love to his very special lady until daybreak and even beyond that.

Epilogue

Delaney's surprise birthday party was a huge success. Tears had sprung into her eyes when she had walked into the darkened ballroom and the lights flashed on and she was suddenly surrounded by family and friends. Even the secretary of state had made an appearance.

And with pure happiness on her face and love shining in her eyes, Delaney had turned to her husband and had given His Highness a thank-you kiss that to Brooke's way of thinking was as passionate as it was priceless.

She had always thought Prince Jamal Ari Yasir was an extremely handsome man and she still thought so, and tonight, dressed in his native Middle Eastern attire, he looked every bit a dashing sheikh. And it was evident that he was deeply in love with his wife. But nothing was more touching than the moment the prince presented his princess with that case of diamonds. She quickly became the envy of every woman in the room. Except one....

Brooke smiled, glancing at the tall, dashing, handsome man at her side. Of course, when Ian's family had seen them together they had begun asking questions. Ian and Brooke hadn't stated the response they had agreed to give earlier. Instead they truthfully and most happily said, "Yes, we're back together and we are planning a June wedding here at the Rolling Cascade."

No one seemed more thrilled with the news than Ian's mom. She had taken Brooke into her arms in a huge hug and whispered into her ear, "I knew he would eventually come to his senses. Welcome to the family, dear."

And speaking of family...

Brooke finally got to meet Uncle Corey's triplets and found that Clint and Cole were two extremely handsome men; typical Westmoreland males. And with her awe-inspiring beauty, Casey Westmoreland was grabbing a lot of male attention.

Brooke also got to meet all the Westmoreland wives. The Claiborne sisters, Jessica and Savannah, married to Chase and Durango. She met Storm's wife, Jayla; and Stone's wife, Madison. Uncle Corey had gripped her in a huge bear hug before introducing her to his new wife, Abby, who was also Madison's mother. Brooke smiled. Talk about keeping things in the family.

After Delaney's party, Ian whisked Brooke off to his conservatory and there on bended knees and under the moon and the stars, he again asked her to be his wife and presented her with a huge diamond engagement ring.

Tears flowed down her face when he slipped the ring on her finger. When he stood up, she looked at him with complete love shining in her eyes. He pulled her into his arms. "I want to kiss you beneath a shooting star," he whispered before trailing kisses along her jaw and neck.

"Do you think we can handle any more passion?" she asked, smiling.

"Oh, I think so. I think that together the two of us can handle just about anything."

And when he leaned down and kissed her, she believed him. Considering all they had been through, they *could* handle just about anything.

* * * * *

"Oh, no!"

The reaction slipped out before Emma Valentine could stop it, for there stood the very man she most wanted to avoid seeing again.

He didn't look any happier to see her.

"Well, come on, get on board," he said gruffly. "I won't bite." One eyebrow rose. "Though I might nibble a little," he added, mostly to amuse himself.

But she wasn't paying any attention to what he was saying. She was staring at him, taking in the royal blue uniform he was wearing, with gold braid and glistening badges decorating the sleeves, epaulettes and an upright collar. Ribbons and medals covered the breast of the short, fitted jacket. A gold-encrusted sabre hung at his side. And suddenly it was clear to her who this man really was.

She gulped wordlessly. Reaching out, he took her elbow and pulled her aboard. The doors slid closed. And finally she found her tongue.

"You…you're the prince."

He nodded, barely glancing at her. "Yes. Of course."

She raised a hand and covered her mouth for a moment. "I should have known."

"Of course you should have. I don't know why you didn't." He punched the ground-floor button to get the elevator moving again, then turned to look down at her. "A relatively bright five-year-old child would have tumbled to the truth right away."

Her shock faded as her indignation at his tone asserted itself. He might be the prince, but he was still just as annoying as he had been earlier that day.

"A relatively bright five-year-old child without a bump on the head from a badly thrown water polo ball, maybe," she said defensively. She wasn't feeling woozy any longer and she wasn't about to let him bully her, no matter how royal he was. "I was unconscious half the time."

"And just clueless the other half, I guess," he said, looking bemused.

The arrogance of the man was really galling.

"I suppose you think your 'royalness' is so obvious it sort of shimmers around you for all to see?" she challenged. "Or better yet, oozes from your pores like…like sweat on a hot day?"

"Something like that," he acknowledged calmly. "Most people tumble to it pretty quickly. In fact, it's hard to hide even when I want to avoid dealing with it."

"Poor baby," she said, still resenting his manner. "I guess that works better with injured people who are half asleep." Looking at him, she felt a strange emotion she couldn't identify. It was as though she wanted to prove something to him, but she wasn't sure what. "And anyway, you know you did your best to fool me," she added.

His brows knit together as though he really didn't know what she was talking about. "I didn't do a thing."

"You told me your name was Monty."

"It is." He shrugged. "I have a lot of names. Some of them are too rude to be spoken to my face, I'm sure." He glanced at her sideways, his hand on the hilt of his sabre. "Perhaps you're contemplating one of those right now."

You bet I am.

That was what she would like to say. But it suddenly occurred to her that she was supposed to be working for this man. If she wanted to keep the job of coronation chef, maybe she'd better keep her opinions to herself. So she clamped her mouth shut, took a deep breath and looked away, trying hard to calm down.

The elevator ground to a halt and the doors slid open laboriously. She moved to step forward, hoping to make her escape, but his hand shot out again and caught her elbow.

"Wait a minute. *You're* a woman," he said, as though that thought had just presented itself to him.

"That's a rare ability for insight you have there, Your Highness," she snapped before she could stop herself. And then she winced. She was going to have to do better than that if she was going to keep this relationship on an even keel.

But he was ignoring her dig. Nodding, he stared at her with a speculative gleam in his golden eyes. "I've been looking for a woman, but you'll do."

She blanched, stiffening. "I'll do for what?"

He made a head gesture in a direction she knew was opposite of where she was going and his grip tightened on her elbow.

"Come with me," he said abruptly, making it an order.

She dug in her heels, thinking fast. She didn't much like orders. "Wait! I can't. I have to get to the kitchen."

"Not yet. I need you."

"You what?" Her breathless gasp of surprise was soft, but she knew he'd heard it.

"I need you," he said firmly. "Oh, don't look so shocked. I'm not planning to throw you into the hay and have my way with you. I need you for something a bit more mundane than that."

She felt color rushing into her cheeks and she silently begged it to stop. Here she was, formless and stodgy in her chef's whites. No makeup, no stiletto heels. Hardly the picture of the femmes fatales he was undoubtedly used to. The likelihood that he would have any carnal interest in her was remote at best. To have him think she was hysterically defending her virtue was humiliating.

"Well, what if I don't want to go with you?" she said in hopes of deflecting his attention from her blush.

"Too bad."

"What?"

Amusement sparkled in his eyes. He was certainly enjoying this. And that only made her more determined to resist him.

"I'm the prince, remember? And we're in the castle. My orders take precedence. It's that old pesky divine rights thing."

Her jaw jutted out. Despite her embarrassment, she couldn't let that pass.

"Over my free will? Never!"

Exasperation filled his face.

"Hey, call out the historians. Someone will write a book about you and your courageous principles." His eyes glittered sardonically. "But in the meantime, Emma Valentine, you're coming with me."

SAVE UP TO $30! SIGN UP TODAY!

The complete guide to your favorite
Harlequin®, Silhouette® and Love Inspired® books.

✓ Newsletter ABSOLUTELY FREE! No purchase necessary.

✓ Valuable coupons for future purchases of Harlequin,
  Silhouette and Love Inspired books in every issue!

✓ Special excerpts & previews in each issue. Learn about all
  the hottest titles before they arrive in stores.

✓ No hassle—mailed directly to your door!

✓ Comes complete with a handy shopping checklist
  so you won't miss out on any titles.

SIGN ME UP TO RECEIVE INSIDE ROMANCE
ABSOLUTELY FREE
(Please print clearly)

_____

Name

_____

Address

_____

City/Town   State/Province   Zip/Postal Code

(098 KKM EJL9)

Please mail this form to:
In the U.S.A.: Inside Romance, P.O. Box 9057, Buffalo, NY 14269-9057
In Canada: Inside Romance, P.O. Box 622, Fort Erie, ON L2A 5X3
OR visit http://www.eHarlequin.com/insideromance

HARLEQUIN®

Super Romance®

ANGELS OF THE BIG SKY
by Roz Denny Fox

(#1368)

Widow Marlee Stein returns to Montana with her
young daughter, ready to help out with Cloud Chasers,
the flying service owned by her brother. When Marlee
takes over piloting duties, she finds herself in conflict
with a client, ranger Wylie Ames. Too bad Marlee's
attracted to a man she doesn't even want to like!

On sale September 2006!

THE CLOUD CHASERS—
Life is looking up.

Watch for the second story in Roz Denny Fox's two-
book series THE CLOUD CHASERS, available in
December 2006.

*Available wherever books are sold, including most
bookstores, supermarkets, discount stores and drugstores.*

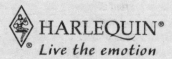

HARLEQUIN®
Live the emotion

If you enjoyed what you just read,
then we've got an offer you can't resist!

Take 2 bestselling love stories FREE!

Plus get a FREE surprise gift!

Clip this page and mail it to Silhouette Reader Service™

IN U.S.A.
3010 Walden Ave.
P.O. Box 1867
Buffalo, N.Y. 14240-1867

IN CANADA
P.O. Box 609
Fort Erie, Ontario
L2A 5X3

YES! Please send me 2 free Silhouette Desire® novels and my free surprise gift. After receiving them, if I don't wish to receive anymore, I can return the shipping statement marked cancel. If I don't cancel, I will receive 6 brand-new novels every month, before they're available in stores! In the U.S.A., bill me at the bargain price of $3.80 plus 25¢ shipping and handling per book and applicable sales tax, if any*. In Canada, bill me at the bargain price of $4.47 plus 25¢ shipping and handling per book and applicable taxes**. That's the complete price and a savings of at least 10% off the cover prices—what a great deal! I understand that accepting the 2 free books and gift places me under no obligation ever to buy any books. I can always return a shipment and cancel at any time. Even if I never buy another book from Silhouette, the 2 free books and gift are mine to keep forever.

225 SDN DZ9F
326 SDN DZ9G

Name	(PLEASE PRINT)	
Address	Apt.#	
City	State/Prov.	Zip/Postal Code

Not valid to current Silhouette Desire® subscribers.

Want to try two free books from another series?
Call 1-800-873-8635 or visit www.morefreebooks.com.

* Terms and prices subject to change without notice. Sales tax applicable in N.Y.
** Canadian residents will be charged applicable provincial taxes and GST.
  All orders subject to approval. Offer limited to one per household.
  ® are registered trademarks owned and used by the trademark owner and or its licensee.

DES04R   ©2004 Harlequin Enterprises Limited

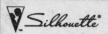

COMING NEXT MONTH

#1747 THE INTERN AFFAIR—Roxanne St. Claire
The Elliotts
This executive has his eye on his intern, but their affair may expose a secret that could unravel their relationship…and the family dynasty.

#1748 HEARTBREAKER—*New York Times* bestselling author Diana Palmer
He was a bachelor through and through…but she could be the one woman to tame this heartbreaker.

#1749 THE ONCE-A-MISTRESS WIFE—Katherine Garbera
Secret Lives of Society Wives
She'd run from their overwhelming passion. Now he's found her—and he's determined to make this mistress his wife.

#1750 THE TEXAN'S HONOR-BOUND PROMISE—Peggy Moreland
A Piece of Texas
Honor demanded he tell her the truth. Desire demanded he first take her to his bed.

#1751 MARRIAGE OF REVENGE—Sheri WhiteFeather
The Trueno Brides
Revenge was their motive for marriage until the stakes became even higher.

#1752 PREGNANT WITH THE FIRST HEIR—Sara Orwig
The Wealthy Ransomes
He will stop at nothing to claim his family's only heir, even if it means marrying a pregnant stranger.

SDCNM0806